Brooklyn's Survival

Dedications

To the beautiful bloggers who go above and beyond to make authors feel the love. You all know who you are and you rock. No matter if you wear hooker heels or dress like a princess you all are beautiful, and I will always be grateful that you were there from the beginning, and will stay with me as long as I write.

To the authors who stood by my side since the beginning. You have been there for every freakout, melt down, ice cream driven hyperactive crazy book talk. You all have become my family. I couldn't have put this book together without you.

To the readers: You all are as loved as my characters. Without you I am merely a crazy person with voices in her head :)

5

Prologue

"It's me you want to hurt, not him. If anyone has to die today, let it be me. Mark deserves better than me. He deserves a wife and babies. He deserves a happy life that ends in old age." I shouted above the gasping audience.

Sirens sounded in the background and the winds picked up as Mark began talking.

"I took her from you," Mark said. "I am the one you want. You already tried to kill me once, and had I not tripped, she would be yours again. If I were dead, what would stop her from going back to you?"

R.J. turned his head to Taylor and pointed the gun at him. Taylor stood with his hands up.

"It was a fantasy," he said. "That was all it was. I stepped up so she didn't have to ask for it. It was one time. She has to choose who she wants to be with, and if she wants to be with Mark, she will. If she wants to be with me, she will. Have you asked her why she is not with you? Have you thought maybe the stack of dead bodies is part of the reason she wouldn't want to be with you? How could she ever trust you not to hurt her?"

I was standing behind the casket, which shielded my waist. R.J. pointed the gun at Mark, who was beside me. Then he pointed it at Taylor, who was moving in on the other side of me. Then the gun returned to me. The sirens grew louder and he was losing patience.

"Let me get you help, R.J.," I implored. "Let Mark take you in, and we can get you what you need." I spoke softly, but the words were all wrong.

"I'm not crazy!" he screamed, just before a shot rang out.

Everything moved in slow motion as my eyes tried to follow the sound of the bullet whizzing through the air. Mark lunged over me and his body jerked as a bullet impacted his chest. The sudden force of the impact knocked him back, as he fell he took me down under him.

"Mark, please don't be dead," I screamed as I pulled and pushed on him to feel that he had no vest on. *Oh, God!* Was he dead?

I squirmed and fought to get loose in a panic. Kate came forward to try and help only for the sound of a second shot to make me jump and work harder to get out from under Mark. It was me he wanted, he could have me if everyone else got to live.

"Kate," I screamed as I looked back up at her. I watched her grab her neck. She went pale as blood poured out through her fingers and she collapsed across from me. *Please God, don't let her die!*

"Mark, wake up," I shouted as I tried to move the two hundred pounds of muscle from on top of me. "Mark, damn it you won't die on me." I pulled and pushed, but he wasn't moving. He didn't make a sound as I punched and hit him trying to get him up.

A shot rang out and my arm burned like fire. I looked up to see that Taylor and RJ were struggling for the gun. I looked down to see blood saturating the ground. It was pouring out of my arm so fast that the grass was no longer green, it had turned a muddy brown.

"Kate, please hold on," I screamed as Kate's eyes closed as she whimpered lightly. The paleness to her said she had lost a lot of blood, and it was pouring out of her as she lay there dying.

"Taylor," I screamed as RJ slammed him back into the casket and it fell open. I lost my breath as I expected my dad to fall out. Shock enveloped me as the only thing in the casket was thousands of forget-me-nots. I watched as the deadheaded blue flowers spilled out like water onto the ground into the blood that surrounded me.

"Help," I screamed as Taylor and RJ continued to fight. Taylor's foot slipped and RJ got the upper hand. They fell and RJ bashed Taylor's head into the casket, knocking him out.

Everything I cared about on the planet was lying injured or bleeding on the ground by the one man who had conquered us all. I took my final breaths as RJ came near me. He kneeled down and placed the hot barrel of the gun to my temple as I shuttered from the coldness he carried.

"I was never alone in this Brooklyn."

Then he pulled the trigger, I heard a click as my eyes clinched tightly, but nothing happened. I gasped and tremors overtook my body as he leaned in and placed his serial killer lips on mine.

"You won the first round, so you got to live, but your friends and father lost. Round two is going to be double the fun."

"Freeze!" Abbott called out as he charged for us. RJ took off running, as the dizziness took me over. The loud sirens came up and the flashing lights blurred in my view. I had lost too much blood and was going to die.

As the darkness overwhelmed me, I knew I would have to *survive* to fight another day.

A Note from theAuthor:

***Please Note that the tone in the book is different from book one. This is because there is no way that a person, even one as strong as Brooklyn will ever be able to be the same after all that she endured in Book one.

I tried to keep it the same, but it made the story superficial. After many hours of talking to personnel in the psychiatric medical field I believe we were able to make her more lifelike in this book after all she has endured.

Read her adventure and find out if Book three will bring her back to who she used to be.

There are only three books in this series.

Chapter 1

Six months later ...

"Hi, welcome to Applebee's is it your first time here?" I asked the couple sitting in the booth in my section.

"No, we come here every Tuesday night for happy hour." The dark haired lady replied with a smile as she pulled her glasses off her head to look at the menu.

"Great! I am Angie, and I will be waiting on you tonight. How about I get you started with something to drink maybe an appetizer to snack on while you are looking over the menu?" I asked and they told me their order.

As I waited for the bartender to finish making their drinks,' I had to wonder. How much more I could take of this life in hiding before I would combust.

I was never an idle person. I was stubborn and creative. I was adventurous and a little quirky. I was Brooklyn until I died. That changed everything for me.

I couldn't take the white walls in the house I was placed in. They were so plain and ordinary, whereas a little bit of color could make me see it in a whole new light. I couldn't stand the fake southern accent I used to try and fit in. I wanted people to think I was from here instead of the Bronx coming out in my speech. I was as fake as Barbie's boobs.

I had no friends, no family and I couldn't get close to anyone for fear they would wind up murdered. Even in hiding I feared for those around me. I still couldn't believe that this is where I wound up, but then again it could always be worse.

After work, I took a shower put on my favorite pink shorts and black tank top. I turned up the radio to rock music and danced around my house until I was exhausted. It was the same thing I did every night. With no friends, no family, and no life there wasn't much else to do.

I looked at a photo of Kate, Mark, and I in a seashell frame that sat on my white stand. It was a photo we had taken at the beach when we took the Jitney to the Hamptons for the weekend.

Mark was holding Kate and I still as a cold wave crashed over us. We were freezing, but the smiles on our faces told the tale of three people who couldn't live or die without each other. I told my friends in the picture goodnight and gave it a kiss. Then I curled up on the couch and drifted off to sleep.

Dream

I was back in the narrow hallway where the white marble floor contrasted with beige walls. I took a few steps forward and heard the click clack echoing from my steps. *This wasn't happening again.*

I knew what was coming and started to run. I needed to get to the red door as I passed all the mahogany ones. I had to get there this time before the dragon threw me into a room.

I ran as sweat enveloped my body and my lungs burned with a need to slow down. I grew tired quickly as the hallway dissolved into water. With each step, a piece of the marble floor broke off and sank into a darkened pit of liquid. I heard Mark's voice bounce off the waving walls saying "Save me Brooklyn" as I tried to keep going.

My adrenaline was not keeping up with me and I was finding myself short of breath and tired. I didn't think I was going to make it as I charged down the hallway trying to get to the door before I became a victim to the bottomless pit beneath me.

Just when I was ready to fall in and sink I saw the red door. I was close enough to have it in my sights as the sound of screams filled the air. A woman screamed as though she was in excruciating pain and her voice echoed off the walls and down the hallway. My heart broke for her as my stomach felt sick.

I was nearly to the door when a serpent head dropped down in front of me from the ceiling above. I had nowhere to go. To be eaten by the snake, fall in the pit, or take my chances with the mahogany door were not the best options, but they were all I had. With no time to decide, I opened the mahogany door and shut it behind me sliding down the door as tears filled my eyes. *I can't let him keep winning.*

The demons always won. RJ always won. There was no way out of the situation I was in. I knew when I looked up there would be an elevator with a light above it. I knew I would be taken up so many stories to be eaten by a man-dragon who steals your soul and never leaves you to rest.

I kept my head in my hands as I tried to calm myself down. I had to accept what would come. I looked up to find myself in the darkened room with only a light shining down showing me I had to get in the elevator. I stood up and turned around to find that the door was gone. I had no choice but to face the devil.

I went to the elevator and pressed the button. The doors opened and as I stepped inside. Suddenly a sheet of glass replaced the doors. I held the wooden rail expecting a rapid decent, but we moved slowly down into the basement of the building.

We came to one floor and it stopped, but the glass didn't open. As the floor lit up, I could see a view of my kitchen from my New York apartment. I saw Mark with some blond, and they were setting the table and happy together.

I watched as they danced around each other as though they had known each other for years. When the blond set the last plate down Mark leaned across the table and placed a kiss on her lips. I banged my fists on the glass when I watched him kiss her and they both looked my way.

"Hello," I spoke softly toward Mark, who only looked at me and smiled. "Why are you in my apartment?" I asked, but they didn't answer. "Why am I here?" I asked as a slithering sound echoed off the walls and sent a chill down my spine.

"They cannot speak Brooklyn," something hissed at me.

"My name is not Brooklyn," I screamed as the elevator descended again. A few floors down I was in the cemetery again and RJ had the gun pointed at us. I screamed and screamed, but it changed nothing as I watched Mark get shot, then Kate, and Taylor was laid out on the ground bleeding profusely from his head. I felt the burn and looked down to see my scar was torn open and bleeding.

As RJ put the gun to my temple, I saw dark shadows come and take my friends souls. I screamed and pleaded with them to stop, but instead I heard the same hissing.

"You can run, but you can't hide. I am in your life, in your head, in your body and in your soul, Brooklyn."

A thick black fog enveloped me and made me cough. I tried to look to see what was happening through the glass, but I couldn't. When the fog cleared, there was no more glass, and I ran out of the elevator. I ran into the darkness until I saw a lit up carousel in the distance.

I tried walking a few steps to hear the click-clack from someone else. My heart leapt into a full charge as I started to run toward the carousel. As I got close, I tripped and fell on the floor. It started cracking beneath me, and the glass floor fell away and dropped me into ice cold water.

I heard a hiss as I swam for the opposite side. I took a sliver of broken glass and kept it in my hand as I climbed out of the water.

The hissing grew louder, as something glowing green moved toward me. As I got closer to the carousel, I could see the walls moving in the light. Then the giant serpent made his presence known.

"What is this?" I shouted as I looked at the children's carousel that would play music so the kids would feel safe as they drove them around and around away from their parents.

"It's your life Brooklyn, climb on."

"I want to know how to get out of here," I demanded holding up the glass at the snake. He gave off a sinister laugh as he backed away from me.

"You have to take a ride and see where you end up. Maybe you will get to go home. Maybe you will die. The journey is up to you."

I climbed on the carousel as blood trickled down my arm from my scar, and out of my hand from the grip I held on the glass. As the carousel started playing a creepy version of the Love Story, I stared at those green eyes until I saw the serpent disappear.

I closed my eyes in relief that he was gone. I took a deep breath and sighed when I felt wind in my hair. I opened my eyes to see everything had disappeared from my life on the carousel. There were no more horses, as I was on the only one. There was no more music, just loud hissing echoing off the waving walls.

My horse stopped going round and round and started on a straightened path right toward the glowing green eyes in the distance. As the horse sped up and fear took over, I shouted.

"I thought you said I got to choose the journey."

"You waited too long so I chose it for you," he hissed and I jumped off the horse into a pit of ice cold water. I swam till I found the edge of the floor and climbed up from the pit. My hair instantly dried as I climbed out and turned from black to blond as snakes formed in the strands. I looked like a Medusa styled Barbie doll on steroids.

"I don't want this!" I screamed, but he lunged for me. I swiped the glass at him and cut his mouth. When he backed off, I lunged for him again slicing his head. *Where the fuck was Rikki Tikki Tavi when you needed him?*

"I love it when you fight back," The snake hissed. "Makes killing you so much fun."

I thought I was winning until his body instantly healed. Then room turned to a burnt orange and the water behind me turned to blood and filled the space with trapped souls screaming out for help.

I reached down and tried to help the blond who was pulling at my leg. I got her half way out of the pool when the she screamed for me to help her.

"Save me Brooklyn," the blond shouted as I tried to pull her out. Something seemed to be holding her in there. I lost her every single time I was here, but this time I had to save her. "Please," she screamed and I grabbed her shoulders and tried to pull. "Only you can save me," she murmured as the life left her face. She turned transparent as her mouth made a silent O.

"I was never in this alone Brooklyn," the serpent said and another snake with gleaming red eyes came up from the bloody hell and was gulping the blond down his throat. I held onto her for as long as I could, but he nearly he nearly took me down as well. I had to let her go. I couldn't breathe and wanted to vomit as I watched her body outline slide down the snake.

I slid back across the floor till I was up against the waving walls as the red-eyed snake slithered out of hell. The larger snake with the green eyes coiled his excessively long tail around my body as I sat there in shock at all the people screaming for help.

"Brooklyn," Mark's voice called out and I looked around as the snake began to constrict. "You should join me. You know we belong together." Mark called out as he walked out of the bloody hell.

"Mark," I screamed, but his eyes turned green and his laugh vibrated the glass floors until they opened up like and earthquake and fire flamed from the pit of hell.

"You can't hide from me. You can't even die to get away from me," Mark said as his face started to change and within seconds I was trapped in the snake's grip as the dragon man stood laughing.

I screamed as he started slowly crushing me. I stabbed him with the glass, but it was too late. The pain was agonizing, as I heard my bones crunch through my screams. Seemed like I lost my will to fight and gave up trying. There was nothing left of Brooklyn inside me. I quickly lost my voice in the darkness as his left head came down and began to swallow me whole.

"Ahh," I screamed as I rolled off the couch. Covered in sweat and scared out of my mind. I took the picture of Mark and Kate and held it close to me as I chanted. "I want to go home."

Chapter 2

A few days later I had finally finished painting my walls and had a little time to spare before going into work. I wiped the paint off my hands and stared at the color. It had taken me five coats to get it exactly the shade I had wanted, and I was once again out of things to do except go to work.

I had painted the living room walls a stormy gray as if it was a rainy New York sky. Besides the one picture, memories were the only thing I had left of the concrete paradise I had to abruptly leave behind.

I wanted so badly to make this hell feel like home. I started with putting color in my life, but sadly it only made me miss seeing the real skyline.

I didn't believe RJ could find me, but I was always on alert just in case. The nightmares were getting better. They ended the second I stopped fighting him, but I was afraid that meant I was losing my will to fight in life.

I walked into the tiny maroon kitchen and opened up the pantry doors to see the newspaper clippings that I was able to scrounge up, and a time line done in yarn. It was RJ's timeline.

Each victim had a set time period between them, and like a winding clock they sped up as I wound him up. The more active he became, the more bodies showed up, and the more public he made their deaths, but his killing methods didn't waiver.

That was the one piece that kept me on guard. There was no way he had a partner, the bodies were too precise and exact to have had two sets of hands on them, but yet those are the words he whispered the day I died.

I didn't let anyone see that I was still working on the case from my memories because they would think I was psychotic, and maybe I was a little, but I assume that is to be expected. After all who can be chased by a killer, tormented, and sent to this hillbilly hell and not turn a little crazy.

I took a deep breath and closed the pantry doors and headed down the hallway and into my room when I stopped to stare at myself in the mirror. I straightened the frame as I studied the blond hair I had been sporting for months. They went to light this time and it made me feel like I looked like Barbie on acid. I was not light and perky so why the hell did my hair have to be?

I showered in my tiny glass shower that was the size of a tall gym locker. I didn't bother to straighten my hair, I merely dried it and let the wavy look take over when I took a brush through my natural curls. I applied minimal makeup on my face and took a deep breath. *Another effing day another effing dollar.*

I walked into the bedroom and laid out my work clothes on the twin sized white sleigh bed I had been given. No more pencil skirts and blazers or courtrooms for me. No, it was a black polo that said Applebee's on the front. I donned my shirt and tucked it into my blue jeans then I pinned on my name tag which lied to everyone.

My name was not Angie and I did not want to take anyone's order. I was Brooklyn, a former A.D.A. forced into hiding because some psycho who probably forgot to take his meds shot me and those I loved. Just thinking back to what my life used to be forced bitterness to grow inside me until anger and weakness were the only emotions I had left.

I finished getting dressed and walked outside in the misting rain. I walked over to the blue Honda Accord that had been furnished for me to get back and forth to work. I swore every time I looked at the car the acidity from my situation grew. It was not like I had privacy anymore as the car was outfitted with cameras, a gps, and an emergency call button. My Marshal, Derrick Stevens had them installed to try and make me feel safer, but it didn't. It had become a bitter reminder that my life would never be my own.

It never seemed to stop raining down here in Texas as the sky began to pour when I got into the car. Every afternoon after a hot sunny morning the rain would come in and give us the added humidity we did not ask for. There were days I thought I might actually melt.

I missed New York. I missed my friends, but no one would tell me if they lived or died. I lived in a state of unknowing, and it was slowly driving me insane.

I walked into work and bypassed everyone saying hello and smiling. I usually was really friendly as I came in, but today was a rough day and I couldn't even fake it. I had my ups and downs and could usually suck it up but as time marched on I was having more bad days than good.

I went straight to the back, dropped my purse and placed my forehead on my locker as my heart was struggling today with not having anyone I could vent to. I took a few deep breaths convinced I would get past this feeling of depression and closed my eyes as I rubbed the reminder on my arm in the shape of a scar.

I looked down to see a cell phone sticking out of the top of Maria's bag. I took a look around and saw no one. I thought about my life and how following the rules and the way my mother raised me led me here. I was always the good girl and yet it got me stuck in a forgotten town surrounded by people I didn't want to know.

I decided to take a page from my dad's rulebook and I pick up the phone and swiped the screen. Thankfully she didn't lock her phone and I was able to pull up Google. I typed in Mark's name first and found a lot of older articles, but nothing since the shooting. Nothing that said he was alive, but no obituary either.

I heard a noise and thought I might get into trouble. I froze to listen. Then when I heard someone coming, I took the phone and bolted for the bathroom. I locked myself into a stall and typed in Kate's name. It mentioned her in the shooting, but nothing more. Once again they had no follow-up, but there was no obituary for her either.

Then I looked for Taylor. He was still the District Attorney in New York County. I was thankful I found him alive, but after six months wouldn't he have wondered where I was?

I then looked up myself and took a deep breath as the thousands of articles flourished. I saw my photo, and a picture of my parents with me. There was an article mentioning me when my uncle Anton was released from prison, but I bypassed reading it when I saw the story of my death.

According to Google the newspapers broke a story six months ago: 'Brooklyn Montgomery died at her father's funeral. She was gunned down by the Cut-Me-Not killer when he spiraled out of control before taking his own life.'

There were only two problems with their story. Deep down I would always be Brooklyn Montgomery, the adventurous, take-no-crap person I was born to be, or at least I would try to be her again.

The second problem was that the Cut-Me-Not killer, RJ, didn't die and he would know I wasn't dead. With neither of us deceased people were at risk of becoming a victim if they ever got close to me.

I rubbed my arm where my scar was that RJ had left when he shot me. I thought about getting a tattoo to cover it up, but the Marshal Service had already absolved everything else about me. All I had left was my necklace from my dad that was a noose, a butterfly tattoo on my ankle, and a scar on my arm.

I had a new name, birthdate, and social security number. They even went so far as to tell me I could only choose between two hair colors. Light brown and blond, those were my choices. Every time I thought about how much freedom I didn't have I wanted to dye my hair blue and show them I was still me, and would do whatever the hell I wanted.

I snuck the phone back into Maria's purse, faked being sick and went home. I had to be at work tomorrow anyway, I could afford one day off. I drove as fast as I could with no real clue on where to go as tears flooded my eyes.

I had wanted to know what had happened, but the truth was bitter. Mark and Kate were most likely dead since there was no mention of them, but Taylor was doing just fine and I was someone that had become a piece of history that no one seemed to even remember. I was nothing to these people anymore.

I grew increasing frustrated with the thoughts of all the good I had done in my life, and all the people I had helped and the only articles about me listed me as dead. Anger was enveloping me as I now knew why no one ever looked for me. I had assumed it was because they were dead, but I was wrong.

"I am not dead," I shouted to no one as I gripped the steering wheel harder. My knuckles turned white as lightning fractured in the sky. The rain was coming down fast and had nowhere to go as it ponded on the road.

I shouted again as the car began to hydroplane. I turned the wheel left as the sudden shift allowed my elbow to knock it out of gear. I tried hitting the brakes, but the car slid sideways. I had as much control over the car as I did my own life. Every memory flashed before me as I was headed straight for a large semi on the side of the road.

I could see Mark's face in my head, he flashed his gorgeous cheek dimples and blue eyes at me as we danced in my living room as Kate entered with Chinese food. I remembered the way he made me feel strong and independent as my car slid over the white line and started to turn so my door would impale the back of the semi. I tightened my grip on the steering wheel once again and closed my eyes.

I thought about how I had always said I would go back. I was always going to kill RJ as vengeance for my father. I was going to capture Mark's heart and never let him go. I was going to be the bridesmaid whenever Kate decided to get married and Taylor and I were going to reclaim New York and only let the innocent run free. I had big plans, but fear kept me rooted, and now my final breaths would be because of a car wreck and not as a last stand in a battle.

I gripped the wheel and held on for impact. I felt the car jerk and my body pull on my seat belt. A sharp blast to my head followed as darkness quickly ensued.

"Ma'am are you okay?" A voice called out as someone banged on the window. I slowly moved my head off the window and tried to look around, but it was painful. I placed my hand on my head and felt wetness. I pulled my hand down and opened my eyes to see blood there. I looked ahead to see I had hit a concrete barrier at the edge of the parking lot entryway just a few feet from the truck. *Fuck that was lucky.* I cracked my window as fear wracked my body because I couldn't see who it was.

"I – I," I couldn't get the words out and the man with the dark hair who was covered in tattoos opened my door and pulled me out as my legs went numb and I couldn't stand up. My head felt like someone had hit me with a sledgehammer, and I wanted to sleep. He held me very firmly against his body where I could not move my head or upper body and shouted orders as rain poured down on me.

"Scooby, get her car into the parking lot before someone hits it."

We got to the door of some shop as lightning cracked and the winds whipped the door open. The man walked through and laid me on a table. He bent over me, inspecting me while he held my neck completely still.

"Ma'am are you all right?" The man with the tattoos asked. I looked around to see that I was inside a tattoo parlor. From the view I had, I could see the back table where they were giving some girl a tattoo on her lower back as she cried to her boyfriend about how much she hated needles.

The room had a warm tone with the darkened red walls and black and white checkered floors. It reminded me of an old 1950s mom and pop shop.

"I am Brook-Angie," I corrected myself as I took a deep breath and tried to push down the fear. He still had not let go of me, but I didn't want him to. It was the closest thing to human contact I had had in a long time.

"Hi Angie my name is Zeke, but most people call me Dizzy," the tattooed man introduced himself as he took a red chair beside me. "Your head is bleeding. How do you feel? Do you know what day it is?" He asked and embarrassment flooded my cheeks.

"I am fine. I just lost control in all the water. I was headed here for ideas on a new tattoo," I lied because I didn't want to admit the truth. He would call emergency services if I told him I felt like my eyes were bulging out of my head as it throbbed along to the beat of my heart that was acting like I had just dropped acid.

"I can call an ambulance if you feel anything out of the ordinary," that was the moment I had to admit nothing felt normal to me. At least not anymore.

"No, I am fine I swear just a little bump," I continued to lie as his tanned face doubled in my vision and then returned to a single blurry version of him. "I was coming here because I heard you were the best when needing an idea for a tattoo."

"What are you looking for? Is it signifying something or are we looking for the next Mona Lisa?" Zeke asked as his brown eyes lit up.

"I want something that signifies internal death."

Zeke looked at me and I could see confusion across his face.

"I am always up for a challenge, but I think you need to give me some details or some idea of what you are thinking of if you want me to draw you some ideas."

I thought about it and explained as much as I could without admitting to anything. Zeke walked over to his area and began drawing. I held a paper towel to my head and waited a bit. I got bored and walked over to the window and saw men pushing my car to get the front bumper off the barrier so they could move it.

I needed an aspirin for my headache, but I would never ask for one because then I wouldn't have a choice as they would call an ambulance and that would start more than I wanted to get into tonight.

A few hours later the rains had cleared, and Zeke had shared the pizza they had ordered with me. He was finishing up a third drawing when the door flew open.

"Where the fuck have you been?" Marshal Derrick Stevens asked loudly.

"I came here to get a tattoo," I whispered as though he was scolding me.

"You didn't think to call me and tell me you wrecked the car?" Derrick glared at me, and I hated that from anyone.

"You are not my father. My daddy died which left me stuck with you," I growled as my head started to throb again.

"You are a spoilt rotten bitch sometimes!"

"Dude talk to her with respect or get the fuck out of my shop," Zeke spoke up as he walked over and handed me a paper. I tuned out the arguing between Derrick and Zeke as I looked down to see he had done it. He had captured exactly what I wanted. It was such a basic concept that I felt guilty wasting his time, but it was what I wanted. Now I needed to find a place to put it.

Derrick went on lecturing me how On Star had to notify him that the car was in an accident because I hadn't called. Zeke argued back with him claiming I had the freedom to do whatever I wanted. If only he knew how much freedom I had truly lost. I couldn't even wreck my car in peace. I just sat with my pounding head listening to them bicker over me.

"Fuck this, brand me already!" I finally shouted over Zeke and Derrick's arguing. It brought the entire room to a halt. "I want this and I know where I want it," I whispered as the whole room looked at me. "I want you to put it where I died," everyone looked at me in confusion except for Derrick. He merely narrowed his eyes at me, but then turned away to answer the phone.

"Be sure that you want to do this sweetie." Zeke whispered and I climbed onto his table. "Don't do it just because you and your old man are fighting."

I merely rolled my eyes. Who would ever think that Derrick was with me?

"I only have one tattoo, a butterfly I got with my best friend Mark when I graduated college. My body is a blank history book and I want to fill it with love and memories. Life doesn't always have good milestones, but that shouldn't stop each of my adventures from having their own page."

Chapter 3

A week later I drove all the way to work with the Marshal's version of security behind me. I don't know why they were following me again. They normally didn't as long as I checked in every now and then, but now they were everywhere. It was suffocating. It would take something creative to get away and get some air, but I knew I was capable. I was after all my father's daughter. If they didn't let up soon, I would be channeling my inner half I got from my dad and taking them on a ride where they would never forget who was actually in charge of my life.

I pulled into the parking lot at work and climbed out of my car. The two Marshals climbed out of their ever-so-obvious black SUV sporting black sunglasses in the rain. I could only shake my head. *This was sadder than a Where's Waldo when someone had previously circled all the Waldo's.*

The Marshals that brought me here knew better. I don't know why they sent rookies to check in on me. Maybe it was because I was such a handful for the others, they would rather torture the newer agents, or maybe it is because I go a little coo-coo sometimes and wind up with a damaged car at tattoo parlours. Maybe Derrick was still angry that I refused a trip to the hospital after my car accident. There were a thousand maybes.

"You guys need to get your shit together," I shouted as the thunder cracked.

"Ma'am?" The younger one yelled back as the winds starting blowing rapidly.

"Sunglasses in a thunderstorm? Stop being so obvious. Just go inside sit down and shut up."

I was carrying my daily irritation on my sleeve for all to see as I walked inside now drenched to the bone. My boss saw me come in and immediately took me to his office.

"Hey Angie, you can't wait on people soaked like that. Take a new shirt and go change, but make sure you bring it back to me."

"Thank you, Todd. It started raining hard as some men in suits asked me for directions outside."

He smiled, as I walked out of the office and into the wood-panelled bathroom to change. There were some perks to being out here in Texas. Like my boss, the friendliest southern guy I had ever met. If it wasn't for him, I would have quit and became a carny.

I returned from the bathroom to find Todd with his tanned skin and cowboy look waiting outside the door. It was a little creepy that he was stalking the bathroom, but I shrugged it off because I knew he meant no harm.

"Hey Angie, there are a couple men in suits requesting you at their table. They are really impatient, so let me have your wet shirt, it will be in a bag in the office and go greet them," I started to walk off when the boss called me again. "Hey Angie if you have any problems, please don't hesitate to get me. You don't have to deal with it alone."

I shook off my boss's speech because I knew it didn't mean what all my brain would imply it to mean. Todd couldn't save me from this life I had been forced into, just like I couldn't stop feeling like some broken down version of myself.

I once saw a therapist who mentioned that traumas change people and it can take years to get back to where they were if they ever get there at all. I refused to listen because in true Brooklyn fashion I always did things on my own timeline and I would not allow years to go by before I felt normal again.

I took my time walking past the bartender nodding to say hi. Noticing a third man, an older man with white hair had joined the two other Marshals. I grabbed my drink napkins and climbed the three steps up to their booth.

"Hi, welcome to Applebee's have you fellas been here before?" I spoke loudly with a fake southern accent.

"Cut the shit." The older one glared at me.

"You are not the one I answer to. Marshal Stevens should be here if there is something he needs to discuss with me." I murmured under my breath so my boss would not hear.

"He is busy dealing with people who actually care about their safety." The older man glared at me. His tone was loud enough Todd must have heard because he was walking over.

"Okay, so that is three cock-sucking-cowboys, and no worries I can double the cock to keep it from burning while it slides down your throat." I spoke loudly and smirked as I walked away.

I walked over to put in their order then waited for the bartender to make the shots as I watched my blond haired cowboy boss make sure I was giving them exemplary service. I made three waters to go with the shots as they were not going to drink alcohol while on duty. As soon as the bartender furnished the order I grabbed a garnish and put everything on a tray and brought them over to the table.

"What is in a cock-sucking-cowboy?" The younger one asked.

"Butterscotch Schnapps and Bailey's Irish Cream," I replied with a wink for the young one. "Just for you, I added a cherry on top," I spoke softly and wanted to laugh as the young one sniffed at the shot. "You fellas figure out what you want?" I asked looking over to see my boss watching me.

"Brook cut the shit. Did you google Taylor Cross?"

I let out a sigh and pretended to write down their order as my boss watched from afar. He usually wasn't looking over my shoulder, but the Marshal's had come in huffy and Todd always wanted to make sure his staff was taken care of.

"Yes, but no one would tell me if any of them were alive. What did you expect me to do? How long did you expect me to wait for an answer?" I whispered as I smiled and pointed down at the menu as if showing them choices.

"What you did was tell the world where you were. For the next couple days get used to us because you won't even pee alone."

"I merely Googled a few names from a phone. I didn't tell anyone anything." I whispered. "It is not like I put it on Facebook."

"Whatever you used, Googled him from the restaurant Wi-Fi as the IP address told us everything. If I can find out that you did this behind our backs, what do you think others can find out? Are you just thick-headed or stupid?"

"It's not my fault. You wouldn't even let me have a cell phone and you watch my internet like teenage boys looking for photos of breasts. *You never take your eyes off the prize.* I asked every single day how my friends were and all you had to do was answer as to if they have a home or a tombstone, but you refused. So, I found one of them. I will find out about the rest and you can kiss my ass. Now, what do you want to eat? I do after all have to work. I speak three languages and have had seven years of college, but the best you boys could get me was Applebee's in the fucking desert!"

"Marshal Stevens please listen," I begged for an ounce of freedom. It had been three days of the Marshal Service following me everywhere. I had enough when one of the women followed me into the bathroom to verify my pee was safe.

"Montgomery, you never listen. You act like a child and throw tantrums. We gave you a new life which means you have to let go of the old one, and until you do we are so far up your ass you will never walk straight again. Are we clear?"

"Fuck you!" I screamed as anger boiled beneath my skin. "I have done everything I was told to do," I bellowed as we circled each other in my living room.

"No, you haven't! You were told that your life was over. You cannot go back, you cannot check on your friends, and you cannot visit your parent's grave. You died!" Marshal Stevens challenged. "Until you are tamed you are stuck with us because you cannot be trusted to do the right thing."

I walked over and punched the wall as I struggled with the anger running through me. I had never been so furious in my life. I pulled my hand back to see my knuckles were bleeding and turning an ugly shade of darkened red as my bones screamed out in pain.

"Come here," Derrick spoke softly as he walked over to my curbside leather couch. He sat down and patted the seat. I walked over holding my hand and sat down beside him.

"Let me see," Derrick spoke softly as he inspected my hand.

"Monte," Derrick yelled and I looked around who the hell was Monte?

"Sir," a man spoke up as he stepped out of my laundry room. *When the hell did he get in there?*

"Ice," Derrick demanded and Monte began going through my kitchen to make a bag of ice and wrapping it in a hand towel. Then Monte handed it to Derrick as Derrick took my hand in his and laid the ice on top.

I felt like an idiot. He was trying to tell me that I didn't listen and threw fits and while I tried to deny it the evidence was now flourishing my skin with shades of crimson and maroon, but to think I wasn't tamed was a sad misinterpretation. I couldn't get any more compliant than I already was. I slid next to him as the ice made it hurt even more. I flinched with every move.

"Monte," Derrick glared at the man standing beside my couch.

"Sir," Monte answered and awaited an order like a soldier.

"Perimeter," Derrick called out and just like that the man was gone into my laundry room and I listened as he opened the window and went out the back. *He could have just used the door.*

"Marshal Stevens, please give me a little space," I whispered as I leaned my head over onto his shoulder.

"No more cell phones," Derrick responded and I refused any acknowledgment.

"I can't keep this up. I feel like my heart is out there in the world walking around looking for me. I welcome death if this is what living without knowing is like."

"Montgomery, it does get easier and I will let up if you can stay away from Google." I nodded that I would, but we both knew I was lying, and I would never let it go.

I had to know how Mark and Kate faired. If they died, I wanted to pay my respects to their graves and gain some closure. If they lived then, I would want to find a way to stay in touch, but I knew that wasn't possible.

"Derrick, most days you are a complete asshole, but you can be nice when you want to be," I groaned with a yawn as I grew comfortable against him. I was never relaxed, and this glimmering moment with Derrick made me feel safe. It was instant exhaustion from all the missing sleep I never got.

"You need a hospital," Derrick muttered ignoring what I had said. "We need to see if you broke your hand," I merely nodded as I drifted off to sleep with my head on his shoulder.

"Tomorrow," I whispered and felt Derrick's arm come down around me as he coddled me. Morning would come and he would be gone, but tonight he allowed me to just breathe.

Chapter 4

The next week I had finally lost my all-day-every-day detail. They were still around, but not overwhelmingly so. I took a shower and straightened my bleach blond hair that I hated. I put on makeup to look like myself for once and put on my uniform. I wrapped my hand which was merely bruised to keep anyone from seeing the remaining discoloration and swelling I was still sporting.

I drove to work and started my shift. I loved the atmosphere that the restaurant brought in. I even loved my boss and this one patron in particular, but none of it could compare to what I felt like when I was home.

Mr. Henderson was my favorite. He was in his early 80s and would sit at one of my tables and tell me about the wars, but not any wars that he had been in. No that would be too easy. He would tell me about defeating Godzilla when King Kong and he became friends. Or how he was the one to catch Nesse the loch ness monster, and how he lured her out with pizza. These days he was hunting for the Abominable snowman in the desert. He would make me laugh and genuinely smile.

The customers came and went. As Todd started letting us go between the lunch and dinner shifts. I began closing down my section even though I still had my one favorite customer waiting to tell me another story.

"Mr. Henderson is there anything else I can get you? I am closing my section out if you have any good stories for me," I spoke sweetly to him and smiled my biggest smile.

"Did I ever tell you how I came across and fought Charlie the Catfish?" Mr. Henderson asked and I laughed.

"No, Mr. Henderson I haven't heard that one," I spoke lightly as I stood by his table.

"Charlie was a six-hundred-pound catfish that swam in the Cumberland River near Paris, Tennessee, and I caught him."

I laughed out loud when envisioning this tiny, frail man trying to lure in a huge fish.

"Mr. Henderson, I think you are telling me a tale. I have never heard of a catfish being that big," I said with a grin.

"Oh he was the biggest catfish in the whole world and I was going to have my picture taken with him, but he broke the stand and fell back in the water just outside of Paris Landing, but I tell you he was so big he could have swallowed me whole."

I laughed and felt at ease for a moment in time. This would have been the type of dad I would have had if my mom hadn't of fallen for a criminal. I had no family and even though Mr. Henderson was merely a customer the bond between us every day at lunch had me grateful that I worked here.

"Mr. Henderson that is a six hundred pound tale," I said as I laughed and shook my head. "Is there anything else I can get you?"

"I'm good, but you better stay out of the water in Tennessee," Mr. Henderson smiled and I laughed.

"Brooklyn," he spoke softly and my smile fell as my breath hitched at my real name being used. I slide into the booth across from the older man as my legs went weak. "I told the man he couldn't be right. I told him your name was Angie, but it's not is it?"

I couldn't speak. I couldn't hear as my heart raced into my ear drums and drowned out everything but its rapid beats. I had to force myself to try and listen to Mr. Henderson as he continued.

"The man came to see me today while you were doing the prep work in the kitchen. He said your name was Brooklyn and he wanted me to give you a message."

I swallowed hard and shoved my anxiety down. I wiped my lip where sweat had broken out and I stayed sitting so my shivers would be minimal to those looking onward.

"Mr. Henderson," I said with the hardest smile I have ever faked. "Is this another story? Cause Brooklyn is a place and my name is Angie."

Mr. Henderson shook his head and pulled out his wallet to pay his check.

"Brooklyn-Angie, whatever your real name is. This is no story. The man with the green eyes sat right here at this table with determination in his tone."

"Green eyes?" I whispered as my lip quivered. I was in full blown panic mode. If RJ was here, then I was as sure as dead. I could envision his tying me up and torturing me as he had done to so many. To watch him slice my skin and watch my blood pour out as I screamed in agony. I could see the premonition of my future if he found me defenseless like I was here and now and it made me sick.

"Brooklyn-Angie, if you are in trouble you know where to find me. I may be old, but I have fought many wars and I ain't done till they put me in the ground."

Mr. Henderson then signed the receipt for his meal leaving me a phone number and an address. Then he stood pulling me up from my seat and wrapped me in his arms.

"Whatever it is, always remember you may not win the first battle or two, but you win the war you fight the hardest," Mr. Henderson whispered in my ear. It made me wonder just how much he really knew from his lunch guest.

"Mr. Henderson," I shouted as he neared the door. "What was the message?" I asked as I walked near him.

"He said to tell you he missed the game."

I kept looking around as paranoia invaded all five of my senses. I could run, and everything said to go, but he would find me. I could fight, but he would win. I needed to call Derrick and tell him, but he would tell me how it was my fault and I didn't need that right now.

On the drive home, I kept thinking how much I hated riddles. They used to be a fun brain teaser and a way to joke around with friends, but when used in a game with no rules and no winners or losers, they sucked. RJ was constantly throwing me clues with his notes, but I never figured them out until it was too late. Today's message wasn't a riddle.

Instead, it was a warning of what was to come.

When I got to my house, I saw a box on my doorstep. I was hopeful it was the taser I had ordered. I picked it up and let myself into the house. I set the box on the floor as I locked all my locks and pushed a chair up against my door. As soon as I secured everything I picked up the box and set it on the table and picked up the landline that had a fifteen-foot cord and called Derrick.

"Stevens," he answered the phone and I nearly choked myself with the phone cord trying to get to the box.

"Hey, it's Brooklyn. Can we meet?" I asked sweetly trying not to give away anything as I cut the tape off the box. I really didn't want to hear the lecture that I knew was coming.

"When?" He really seemed to love short answers and was as unfriendly as they came sometimes, but I assume it came with the job as everyone he worked with had a target on their backs.

"I am off the rest of today."

"Why?" Marshal Stevens replied.

"I would rather discuss that with you here," I retorted as I opened the box there was a mahogany cigar box inside.

"Talk!" Stevens demanded me to tell him over the phone as I opened the cigar box to find a photo of my dad's funeral. RJ was kneeling and had the gun to my temple. It was taken from the seating area where my family had been. My body started the tremors all over again, and my breathing became erratic as I lifted the photo to see a finger laying inside a Ziploc bag of ice that had barely melted.

"Brooklyn, you there?" I heard Marshal Stevens voice say as I dropped the phone. "Montgomery answer me."

I picked up the little note card that said 'Miss me?' on the front when I pushed it open a blue forget me not fell out and my heart skipped a beat.

Reminder

I wanted you to have
a
piece of your daddy.

As the clock goes
tick-tock
toward our time
together.

"Fuck," he had found me, and I had led him here by searching out my friends. I just know I had done this to myself, or he would have made himself known long before now.

The police and the marshals were breaking down my door within minutes. With guns drawn they covered the house and the area around the house. I sank to the floor and cried into my knees, as I just wanted to end this. I was at my breaking point with it all.

I was miserable in witness protection. I never let anyone get close to me for fear it would end their life. I lived my life constantly looking over my shoulder, and I questioned every morning if that would be the last time I saw the sunrise. I couldn't do it anymore.

"Brooklyn?" Marshal Stevens crouched down to sit in front of me so I was looking at him eye to eye. "In light of this I think it would be best if we move you again, tonight."

"He will just find me again," I whispered as the tears fell from my eyes. I was actually beginning to wonder if the blade of RJ's knife would be any worse than the position I was in now.

"He won't find you this time," Derrick replied and held out his hand to get me off the floor. I took it and stood up. "Don't give up on me Brooklyn. I can keep you safe,"

Derrick whispered in my ear. I gave him a half smile as I walked over and took the picture from my coffee table, and walked out the door.

"Where are we going this time?" I asked in a whisper as I climbed into the back of the Marshal's SUV.

"Do you have a preference?" Derrick asked and I thought about it.

"I hear there is great fishing in Tennessee," I replied and Derrick's brows drew together. He looked at me as though I was up to something, but I wasn't.

"Since when do you fish?" Derrick asked and I shrugged my shoulders.

"I don't," I replied and he shook his head. After a couple of minutes of phone calls and texts Derrick replied.

"Your new name will be Morgan, and we are headed to Nashville."

Chapter 5

Three months later ...

"Hi welcome to Demo's, have you been here before?" I asked the patrons as the darkened Italian restaurant filled up. Everyone was wearing yellow and blue and sporting pride for the Nashville Predators. I had never been to a hockey game, but some of the girls were headed there after work, and I thought I might tag along, but was really uneasy with the thought of being outside. I thought I had taken steps in reclaiming my life, but it seemed that seeing my dad's finger took me a few steps back into hibernation.

"Hey, Morgan," My boss Kevin called out. "When you get a minute come see me," I didn't like the sound of that so I took their drink orders and headed straight for my boss.

"Kevin," I spoke softly as I entered his white bricked office behind the kitchen.

"Hey I know you are still kind of new, and getting the hang of things, but how do you feel about taking on a large party? Stacy went home sick, and we are short-handed. If I get Rachel to back you up, would you want to try out a large party?"

"Sure," I replied and Kevin smiled and almost seemed relieved. I went back to the dining area and made my tables drinks.

As time got closer, I watched as they kept the area cleared and soon began pulling tables together. The way they took people around the area and allowed it to be open reminded me of a crime scene. The tables were the body and the area was branded with invisible crime scene tape that no one would cross. *God, I missed my life.*

Everywhere I looked was a reminder of things I would never do again. I eventually crossed the line and flourished the table with hot bread and water so they would have something until their entire party was there.

"Hi I am Morgan I will be your server tonight what can I get you started with?" I asked as the first couple arrived at the tables. Soon all the tables were filled except for four chairs in the middle.

Everyone was overly excited that their friend was being proposed to in her hometown. I soaked up all the conversation I could and went back into the kitchen to put in the kids orders who were not wanting to wait for the guests to arrive.

"Hey Morgan," Rachel spoke up in the kitchen. "How are you doing with the party? Need anything?" She asked.

"No, I am good. Just waiting for the last of the party to arrive."

"I think they just arrived if you need anything let me know I only have two tables now," Rachel smiled and I began dressing the plates to deliver out to the kids.

When I walked out they were all hugging each other so I slid in and placed the kid's food down and then walked away so I could give them some time to settle in before taking the rest of their order.

"What did you do?" Rachel asked as she entered the kitchen only minutes later.

"What?"

"The man who just came in wants to see the manager. What did you do?" Rachel asked again.

"Nothing," I spoke up but fear invaded my core. What if they were mad the kids got their food first or because I didn't stay and take their order. I couldn't lose this job. It was so expensive trying to make it on tips and I needed this job or Marshal Derrick would be back up my ass again. "Will you go find out?" I pleaded and Rachel nodded.

"Stay in here, and I will be right back."

I helped in the kitchen while I waited. The seconds seemed to take years to go by until I saw Kevin come back into the kitchen.

"Hey Morgan, I asked Rachel to take their orders so I could talk to you." I swallowed hard and prepared myself to apologize for whatever I had done. "A man came in and asked that I give you this for your birthday. You should have told me I would have never asked you to stay late on your birthday," I looked at Todd in confusion, but I took the blue gift bag and pulled out the paper. Hundreds of blue forget-me-nots fell to the floor.

"I think I am going to be sick," I spoke aloud and Kevin sent me to his office to sit down for a minute. I didn't know what to do so I picked up a kitchen knife on my way into the office and held it tight. I took my phone out of my apron, before the tremors in my hands could stop me from dialing a number.

"Stevens," Derrick answered, but I couldn't speak. "Montgomery?" He asked and I could only whimper. I heard the rapid snapping of fingers and soon I heard engines coming to life. "I am coming to you, do not hang up, the car is tracking the gps in your phone."

I sat the phone on the desk and held the knife tightly in one hand as I looked inside the bag to see there was nothing in the bag but the flowers. There was no note or warning, just the flowers. I swallowed hard as it was just another riddle or a warning that I wouldn't understand until it was too late.

It was a matter of minutes before Derrick had the area swarming with normally clothed marshals. They sat at the bar, they sat in the booths, and they were pacing the sidewalk outside.

Derrick walked into the office and knelt down in front of me with his brown bedroom eyes and said the words I didn't want to hear.

"I think we should move you again," but I wasn't going this time. They could send me to Timbuctoo, but RJ had some kind of tracker where he was able to find me. I didn't know how, but I wasn't going to go through this again.

"Derrick, I want to go home," I spoke softly, but with confidence so he would understand how serious I was. He pulled a number out of his pocket and handed it to me. I looked at it, it was a New York number, but not one I recognized.

"I think you are just homesick. Make this call, swear them to secrecy, and then say goodbye. Say what you need to because we are going to destroy your phone as soon as you hang up. I am giving you this in hopes you will let me move you somewhere else, and not risk their lives."

My forehead crinkled in confusion as I dialed the number and let it ring.

"Hello." A male voice came on the line. I stayed quiet while I placed the voice. "Who is this?" I figured out who it was.

I started singing my own version of "Akineyle's Put it in your mouth" and he laughed. It was a rap song that after one too many fireballs we created our own lyrics for it.

"Brooklyn? Is that you?" Eddie asked and I could hear Kate in the background "Hang up and come finish yoga with me," I nearly burst out laughing that she had him doing yoga in my absence. Tears then filled my eyes as I could hear my best friend whom I had thought died that awful day.

"Yeah, it's me. Let me talk to her," I said as my voice quivered.

"Kate you should pause the yoga and take the call," Eddie called out.

"Who is it, babe?" Kate replied.

"Just take the phone," Eddie murmured and I waited impatiently for her to take the phone.

"Hello," Kate spoke softly. I nearly imagined the questions she would have for me, but none of the answers she would want. As much as I wanted this I was afraid of the outcome.

Would we still be friends? Was I putting her in danger? What happens if RJ goes after her because I called her? There were so many questions, but I selfishly didn't care because I needed her like I needed water to stay hydrated.

"I am calling from outside the house," I whispered our running joke from before everything went down.

"I am answering from inside the house," Kate replied and I heard her gasp. "Is it really you? They said you were dead," Kate's voice quivered. Derrick squeezed my knee and stood up to walk to the door.

"With the life the marshals have given me, I might as well be dead. I miss you, Kate. How is you? Taylor?" I gulped down my fear because I knew Kate held the key to finding out if Mark was dead. "How is Mark?" I couldn't stop the tears from cascading down my cheeks as I heard Kate quietly sob into the phone. Derrick stood in the doorway and listened to my phone call. I always envisioned finding my friends alive and in my head I knew what to say and do, but this was so much harder than I thought it would be.

"Where have you been? Can I see you?" Kate asked as she sniffled into the phone. I so wanted to answer her. I wanted to tell her to meet me and lose my security detail like I had done a hundred times before, but it was different now. I was different.

"I can't tell you, but I will say I am coming home," I spoke softly and Derrick's face fell. He looked at me with concern and aggravation. He just didn't understand, if I had to be hunted and eventually killed. I wanted to die surrounded by my family and friends. I tilted my head and gave Derrick a look that said I was sorry, then returned to my conversation. "Now how is Mark? Taylor? You?"

"Well let's see. I got shot, spent ten days in the hospital to wake up and be told my best friend was dead. So for me it has been a really shitty year. Taylor got a concussion and a fractured eye socket, but he returned to work as if nothing had happened. I think that man's injuries run deeper than any of us know. He is like a machine. All he does is work, but he is turned goofy. He makes jokes that aren't funny all the time. I call him from time to time to make sure he is okay, but he isn't. We all took your death hard. Your funeral was beautiful. Taylor brought your uncle Anton out of prison and gave him probation to finish the last year of his sentence to handle your affairs."

"I had a funeral, and no one thought to look inside the casket?"

"Brooklyn seriously they said he shot you in the head. We wanted to remember you as you were, not with a hole in your head. Your uncle has been paying the lease on your apartment every month because none of us could stomach going through your things. We just packed up your stuff and put it in storage about a month ago, but the apartment is empty and your uncle still holds the lease. It was hard for any of us to go in there and we weren't really sure what to do with your things. I know we talked about RJ and what happens if he found you, but we never talked about what happens when you die."

I started pacing the office waiting to hear about Mark. The man who tried to shield me with his body as he took the bullet that was meant for me. I loved that man more than life itself but had hurt him so badly. I said a prayer every day that he would be all right.

"Kate, how is he?" I asked because she had stopped talking. I was scared of the answer, but had to know. I could hear the quiver in her voice and the shaking of her breath. She was crying again.

"He is alive, Brooklyn," I heard a rush of air escape her and knew I wasn't going to like what came next. "Brook, you hurt him really bad before the shooting. Even after that he loved you enough that he took a bullet for you and felt the grief because he still couldn't save you. He took your death the hardest."

"What does that mean Kate?"

"Brooklyn, I won't go into how he was after you died, but he is not the same man. He dropped homicide and is now working over at narcotics. He threw himself into work and-."

There was a pause and a tear rolled down my face.

"I think you should go see him as soon as you are home. When will you be here?"

The phone call with Kate was as relieving as it was gut-wrenching. After hanging up with Kate, I looked at Derrick and without another thought in my head I spoke the statement we both knew was coming.

"Pack a bag Derrick, because I am going home with or without you and the service keeping me safe."

Chapter Six

I loved the city. The chaotic atmosphere, the crowds, the traffic, and the constant loud noises were things I had missed about New York. It had taken four days to get here, and worth every agonizing second.

I stared ahead at the concrete skyline as we drove into the city. The marshals had insisted that they tag along an extra day or two as I left their protection. Normally people didn't leave the Marshal Service outside of a body bag so they were concerned if they left I would change my mind or that the inevitable would happen the second they dropped me off.

We entered the Lincoln tunnel as the sun was rising. The smell of exhaust overwhelmed my senses in the tunnel as my eyes watched the yellow lights pass us by. The sound of cars honking filled my ears. It was done out of habit and not as if it would make traffic move. As my nerves tingled in delight, I could finally sigh and lay my head on Derrick's shoulder because he had brought me back home.

By the time, we got through early morning rush hour traffic and made it to my apartment complex in Tribeca. I had taken a nap in the SUV.

The Marshals cleared the building before allowing me out of the vehicle. Then I was escorted up the elevator and to my apartment door. The locks had been changed and there were added deadbolts to the door.

"It is good to see you again Miss Montgomery," my old manager Tony spoke softly as Derrick took the key from him.

"Spasibo," I replied thanking him in Russian. Tony was in charge of three separate apartment complexes that sat side by side on the street. He was an elderly man with a Russian accent who had lived in the apartments as long as I had known him.

"I thought you didn't speak Russian," Derrick whispered as he started unlocking the different deadbolts.

"I am not fluent, but I know a little," I smiled as my excitement grew with knowing I was finally home. I was thrilled to talk in my father's native tongue and be known as Brooklyn. I still had to lose the Barbie blond strands, but one thing at a time.

I had refused a new home. This was my place and I was not going to let some killer send me into hiding anymore. At least that is what I told myself when in reality the lease was paid and my savings from my time in Tennessee wouldn't pay for half a month's rent in any New York apartment. I took a deep breath, closed my eyes and opened the door to walk into my new life.

I looked at my open floor plan apartment with the light walls and darkened hardwood floors. I had picked all the features out myself, and I loved every inch of it. I missed my home. I could stare at the island and remember when Mark cooked for me and did other things to me that made me smile. I could look at my navy blue couch and remember when Kate had too much to drink and would crash there.

The apartment was once again filled with boxes that were stacked three high and lined the walls. It was as if the last year and a half was non-existent. This time eighteen months ago I was moving in here and starting a new job, which isn't so different than where I was now.

"Brooklyn," I heard a familiar voice call my name and smiled as Kate came out of my bedroom. The Marshal's drew their guns to aim at Kate. She put her hands up in defense as they warned her not to move.

I glanced over at Derrick and gave him a smile as I motioned for them to put the guns down. As soon as they did I sprinted for her and wrapped my arms around her. I wanted to cry in relief that I had my friend back.

"Oh my, you are really blond," Kate said as she pulled back and played with the ends of my hair. Then she pulled me back in for another hug. Now that she had gotten her two cents in about my hair she let her feelings shine as she held me so tightly to her that I was losing my breath.

"Eddie and I moved everything your uncle had in storage back in the apartment," Kate whispered in my ear and then pulled back to look me in the eye. "I didn't know what to say so your uncle knows you are returning and what's happened. I hope that is okay," Kate didn't wait for an answer as she pulled her back to her roughly as tears filled her eyes. "It is so good to see you, honey. I missed you. You can't ever die on me again."

"Miss Montgomery we need to go over a few things," Marshal Stevens said and I pulled out of Kate's arms to see the tears flowing down her cheeks.

"We are no longer going to be looking after you, by your choice. I am going to need you to sign some documentation to that effect."

I nodded my head and wiped the tears from my eyes as Kate held my hand and the Marshals continued their speech about what they wouldn't do since I was ending my save-my-life care.

"Marshal Stevens she will be fine because I won't let anything happen to her," Kate spoke up when they started going over the risks I was taking.

"Miss Montgomery, you do know what you are doing, right? You have thought this through? You can always come back with us, and we can place you somewhere else. It is not too late."

I thought it was sweet the way Marshal Stevens actually looked concerned. His brown bedroom eyes said that he was worried, while his tanned facial expression said he was just doing his job.

"Marshal Stevens, please understand that this is not about the safety and supervision you and your men have given me. This is about my need to take my life back. I lost my spine when my father died and have allowed everyone else to make my decisions. It is time I stood on my own two feet and fought back. I may not get back to being me right away, but I will get there, and I can't do that in hiding."

"Miss Montgomery-," he started again and I merely put my hand up to stop him.

"If I should die on this journey at the hands of RJ. Then that is my fate, but a wise person told me that I could lose a battle and still win a war. I lost the battle at the cemetery and have coward in the corner ever since. It is time for me to stand up and win the war not only for myself, my friends, and my family but for the victims. I should have done it a year ago instead of being taken into custody."

"Miss Montgomery, I can appreciate your new found freedom and voice, but I was going to say it is your decision and please call me Derrick. As I am no longer your Marshal." He motioned for the men to clear out and leaned into me as he spoke quietly. "I don't feel good about this so I am going to stick around an extra week just in case you change your mind. I will be at the Marquis."

Memories flooded me with the mention of that particular hotel. I went to shake his hand and he pulled me in for a hug. Looked like Mr. one-word-response-man was going to miss me. I couldn't help but smile as I hugged him with one arm as Kate would not let go of my hand. It had been a really long time since I felt like I was cared for, and now I was basking in it.

He released me and slid his card into my hand before turning and walking out of my apartment. The butterflies had taken root in my stomach as I tasted freedom for the first time in what felt like a really long time. At this moment, I was no longer under anyone's thumb and it was invigorating.

"Are you tired? Do you want to rest? Do you want me to order Chinese, and help unpack?" Kate asked and I shook my head. "What do you want to do first?" Kate asked as she made a crooked smile and played with the blond hairs I was sporting.

"Do you think I could get a spa appointment today? I can't do blond anymore."

"Sure it will be my treat, let's go," Kate said as she grabbed her purse and then she grabbed a black box. "You might feel better with this," she stated as I took the box and opened it to see my 9mm Sig Suer Liberty Edition gun in its holster waiting for me.

"I can't conceal carry in the state of New York," I spoke with a whisper as I held back tears from the overwhelming emotion I was feeling being back home, and seeing my gun. I turned to see the inscription on the slide said "Lyubov moya," it meant my love in Russian. It was what my dad always called me. I suddenly missed him as if his death was new.

"You can with this," Kate spoke softly and handed me my A.D.A. badge.

"Kate I am not an Assistant District Attorney anymore."

"Brook you fucking died!" Kate scoffed at me as if in disbelief. "Don't you think it is time you learned to break some rules to save your own ass?"

Kate put her hands on her hips and paced as though she was anxious about being here with me.

"You wear it, use it only if you have to, and if anyone questions it, we lie our asses off."

"Kate," I started to say, she didn't have to go out with me if it was going to cause her anxiety, but she was Kate and never listened to anything I had to say ever.

"I have no doubt when Taylor sees you he will give you your job back. That man was head over heels for you a year ago and I have no doubt there is something still there for him," Kate spoke softly as she seemed to lasso in her emotions. *I can't imagine how hard this is for her.*

I put my holster on the waist of my jeans and checked the clip to see it was empty. My mind flashed to the moment Mark came in and I was in Taylor's lap kissing him. That heart-wrenching moment when I had to pull my gun on Mark to keep him from hurting Taylor.

I remembered watching through the tears as he unloaded my gun one bullet at a time and placed them on my desk. That was the moment he broke my heart and told me it was over. I had to shake the memory from my thoughts as I was already on emotional overload with finally getting what I craved for months. I had my freedom and I was going to enjoy it.

"I didn't know how to load it so the bullets are in the bottom."

I looked inside the box and there they laid all seven bullets. I loaded the six into the clip and pushed it up into the handle. Slid back the slide to put one in the chamber. Then I pulled the clip out and added the one remaining bullet.

I loved the feel of the gun in my hand. It was like a long lost friend. It had stayed by my side while we had been through so much together, and without the marshal's overlooking my every move this would be my safety. If I would have had it at my dad's funeral, my life would have turned out so differently.

"I need to find a way to see Taylor and Mark without coming to them as the walking dead."

"There really is no way to prepare them, Brooklyn," Kate spoke softly, and I knew she was right, but I didn't want to just show up alive. "I think maybe we need to get you a cell phone and then stop by Taylor's office and get your job back. Then we can fix your hair. That way Mark won't arrest you for having the gun. He is a different person and is strictly by the books."

I finished getting my stuff together and walked out the door with Kate. She ignored me most of the cab ride as she was calling and making appointments for me to get my hair, and nails done. She was even booking me a massage. *God, I missed this woman!*

After getting a new phone on her plan as *Morgan* didn't have much credit history. I walked up to the security office and showed them an ID that said my name was Morgan Clark. I didn't have any other ID, which was fine because as far as the press knew Brooklyn Montgomery was dead anyway.

Kate and I rode up the elevator that made me uneasy and headed down the gray corridor toward Taylor's office.

"Hey Kate," I stopped her and pulled her aside. "Let me go in there alone. Please. I think this would go better if it were just me."

"You nervous?" She asked and I nodded my head as I wiped my sweaty palms on my jeans. "

I will give you a few and then come join you. It has been a hot minute since I saw Taylor and want to stick my head in and say hello."

I nodded my head and headed to the end of the hallway. I walked slowly as I saw my old office. I stared at the familiar sight as I approached the open door, and upon instinct I walked inside the now forgotten room.

Nothing had been moved. The office was still the same. As I rounded the desk and rubbed my finger through the dust, I saw a photo of my mom and dad. The Cut-Me-Not files were still on my desk waiting for an update. This stopped being an office and became more of a time capsule. Leaving my office in such a manner was a testament to how people hadn't moved on since my death. *I hated knowing I had hurt people.*

When the last A.D.A. died I came in like a bat out of hell and took over her office and forced life to move on around me, but from the looks of my office no one had replaced me or even cleaned in here. I was starting to question how Taylor would take my return.

As dread overwhelmed me, my nerves kicked in and my palms grew sweaty as I conjured every possible scenario in my mind. The only thing I could do is go knock on his office door, and find out. I exited my old office and walked the fifteen feet to his door.

I stood frozen as I heard him bellow angrily through the door. I told myself to just knock on the door, but fear kept me rooted in place. I convinced myself it would be fine and lifted my hand to knock when he grew quiet for a moment, but I couldn't. I turned to walk away when I heard him yell through the door.

"We haven't had a body there in a year. It is not cursed. Make the damn food and have it delivered by someone else if you have to!"

When he was quiet for a moment, curiosity took over and I lightly knocked, but he started talking loudly to whomever he was speaking to again. I slowly opened the mahogany door to find him staring out his glass window with the phone to his ear.

"No, I said the third Saturday! Not Friday, not Sunday. I want it there at the ball on the 24th the third Saturday. I don't care about the anniversary!"

I cleared my throat and watched as Taylor held up a finger without spinning around to see who I was. From his stance, he needed a shoulder rub. He sounded stressed and it was wearing on him as he rubbed the back of his neck.

"Fine, see that you do that then, and be on time!"

He turned and slammed down the phone on his cherry wood coloured desk and started shuffling papers without even looking at me. He was overloaded with work from all the files laying on his desk. *Was he taking on every case?*

"Now that you have breached my office without being told to come in how can I help you?"

I stayed quiet for a moment and was going to talk, but what could I say? In this very moment I knew I should say hi or apologize or something. I was better than this. I should have had a plan. I was speechless.

"Look whatever you are selling I am not buying. Whatever case I am handling does not get discussed without an appointment, and,-" his words froze as he looked up at me. His eyes narrowed and he looked at me from head to toe. I thought he was in shock, until he grazed my body again and paused on my badge sitting right beside my gun on my jeans. Then he smirked as he noticed my gun.

"You know carrying a concealed weapon is illegal in the state of New York."

I nodded my head, but was frozen in place. I was still at a loss for words, and couldn't tell if he was happy to see me or angry.

"Well, well aren't you the good girl? The one who defied the odds to be the opposite of her dad?" I nodded my head with a smirk. "Since when do you break the rules?" He asked and I gave him a huge smile. His face lit up as he came around the desk and wrapped me in his arms.

"Since breaking the rules brought me back from the dead," I said as I hugged him. He held on tight as if I could disappear and I swore I heard a sniffle, but Taylor never let anything but happiness show. Now would come the hard part. The apologies I would have to make and questions he would surely have.

"How long are you here?" He asked as his eyes danced with delight in seeing me.

"As long as I live and breathe."

Chapter Seven

I spent an hour talking to Taylor until he had to go to court and answered everything I could although I was unsure on if I could tell him who I had been and where I had been.

I was almost thankful when he had to leave because it was exhausting rehashing all that had happened while carefully wording things. He really was a different man now, but then again it could be my perception of him as I am no longer the same person either.

Taylor's personality was still there, but it seemed as though he didn't take much seriously anymore. He would ask a dozen questions before I got one answered and then would make a joke that carried no humor. Maybe it was the shock of my return or maybe I made him uncomfortable.

Taylor had agreed to talk about me returning to my position to some higher-ups, but I had a temporary job at his office until they decided. Neither one of us knew what the protocol was to return from the dead inside the District Attorney's office. He took my badge but left me my gun. Taylor had played such a small role in my life, but in the end he had found himself a place in my heart.

I had to pry Kate off her cell phone with Eddie to get her to head to the precinct. She had forgotten Taylor and me as she sat in the empty conference room flirting on her phone. I guess I would have to cut Eddie some slack because she really did look happy.

A twenty-minute cab ride took us to the police department. I climbed out of the car and my stomach fluttered as I stood outside the police department. I felt sick when I remembered walking this same sidewalk without fear, without a care in the world when I had found my father dead in his home. I remember the numbness I felt for everyone and everything.

I had been this adventurous person who did things her own way to have the breath knocked out of her and suddenly I am too scared to live for myself. It needed to stop. I needed to find myself again. No matter what it took, I was going to get the last year of my life back and move forward as if RJ never existed.

Kate went inside to invite Mark to lunch. I didn't know how to re-introduce myself to Mark. He was my heart and soul. He was still the love of my life, and I honestly didn't know how he would take my return. I couldn't imagine what I would do if my mom or dad just showed up on my doorstep.

I watched the people walk back and forth in front of me. I was careful to keep an eye out for anyone or anything out of the ordinary. Twice I thought I saw RJ, but the green eyes just kept walking. I had to get a grip on the anxiety I was harbouring when in public.

I paced the sidewalk as my nerves flared. My body was having a competition between the butterflies in my stomach and the pulse of my heart. I think I was going to puke before I even saw him. What if he hated me? What if he had moved on? What if he wished I was dead?

I had to shake the questions from my mind as I heard Kate coming as her laughter carried through the doorway. I watched as Mark came out of the police department smiling at something Kate had said.

"I am glad to hear Eddie passed his exam," Mark stated as I took in the back of him.

"He was so excited. He said we all have to celebrate his new job soon," Kate smiled at Mark and looked behind him and winked at me.

"Hey Mark, I need to-," Kate started but was cut off by another voice.

"Hey honey wait up," I saw a woman run up and wrap her arms around Mark and hang on his side. My eyes stared in disbelief as she was the blond. She played a role in every nightmare I had. I was always trying to save her and I always failed.

Suddenly, I couldn't breathe as I took in her appearance. She had blond hair and green eyes with long legs. She had alabaster skin like mine was before my journey to the southern states left a light tan behind. She looked like she was athletic and stared at Mark like he was her world. *Oh God, I had been replaced.* I felt sick and turned to walk away as quickly as I could.

"Hey," Kate screamed as I crossed the street without looking only to get honked at. "Stop," Kate screamed and I tried to run away.

"Stop!" Mark called out. I could hear his loud stomp coming up behind me quickly. I put my hand over my gun and froze, whether it was fear or anxiety I will never know because I immediately did as he told me to in his alpha tone.

I stopped right where I was, holding my breath and listened to the man speak. "NYPD!

Stop, move your hand away from the gun and show me some identification."

"Mark, wait," I heard Kate yell. I didn't bother to turn around. I closed my eyes and revelled in the warmth and comfort that exuded from Mark. I tried to soak up all I could, as it had been a long time since I had felt that pull to him. "Mark, put the gun down and stop making a scene," Kate muttered. She walked around the front of me to see that an involuntary tear was falling down my face as I moved my hand off my gun.

Seeing Mark with some blond hanging off his hip was the punch in the gut I needed to see that the fantasies of my return were not what was going to happen. I swallowed hard as I got ready to say hello and goodbye to the love of my life.

"Hey guys wait up," the female voice said behind me. "What is going on?" She asked and I sent a pleading look to Kate to just let me walk away, but she ignored it. Was I ready for this? Was I strong enough for this?

"Hey Maya, do me a favor can you run back in and see if I left my cell phone on Mark's couch. I hate walking in there. They look at me weird," Kate stated with a wink at me. *Oh God, please let me just walk away.*

"Sure thing Katie. I will be right back."

I heard retreating footsteps as we stood in the road as cars finagled around us. I tried to take a step forward and got as far as the sidewalk before Kate held up her hand.

"I hate when she calls me Katie. I am not five years old Mark," Kate huffed as she placed her hands on her hips.

"Kate you have never given Maya a chance. I know she will never be your best friend, but try to be nice," Mark growled out his words and Kate ignored it and moved on with the conversation.

"Now that we have a moment I would like you to meet my friend," Kate said with a sarcastic tone. "I wanted you to meet her alone. I didn't know the gold digger would be present today. Must be payday," Kate replied and I couldn't help but want to laugh.

Kate was always defensive of me, and she never had a problem telling people exactly what she thought when the idea popped into her head.

"Kate, I am warning you. I don't know what crawled up your ass today, but if we are going to lunch you will behave."

"We'll see about that," Kate retorted and then her eyes flashed over to mine and my smile fell as I knew what she was about to do. "Mark, I would like you to meet my friend."

"Maybe I could if she turned around and looked at me and used her voice to introduce herself," Mark stated matching Kate's sarcasm. I wanted to throw up as I silently murmured the word please over and over again, but Kate just ignored me.

"Mark, I believe you know my best friend Brooklyn Montgomery," Kate said and I could feel the instant tension in the air. It was thick with disbelief and anger surrounded me. I could almost hear the fury boiling up inside Mark as his breathing had changed at the mere mention of my name. I hung my head as I tried not to cry.

"Do I need to call you someone because you are seeing shit?" I heard the exasperation in his voice. His instant rage told me this man was still hurting from my death. "We were both there or don't you remember sitting front row at her funeral?"

Kate took Mark's anger with grace as her face never faltered. I could almost hear him grinding his teeth as his agitation rose to the surface at the mention of my name.

"Mark, wait," Kate called out, as Mark started to leave.

"You know what, fuck this," Mark returned and pointed his finger in Kate's face. A few more steps and he would see my face. "I know you don't like Maya, but Brooklyn is gone and bringing someone to impersonate her would have worked better if you got her right! She doesn't even have to face me for me to know it is not her. This girl is too skinny, has the wrong skin tone, hair color, and she is not Brooklyn."

Mark turned to storm off but had to have that last little comment before he left.

"I loved Brooklyn, and to bring her up when I am finally happy is beyond wrong, Kate. Don't come around us again. Maya already feels like she is living in Brooklyn's shadow and you are not helping."

"Mark please wait," Kate called out as I heard his feet start to walk away again. "Mark please just give me a moment," Kate pleaded and then looked at me. "You have to tell him," she whispered to me. I shook my head lightly.

"She has to tell me what?" Mark growled as his patience was wearing thin.

"Mark do not overreact," Kate said and I took a deep breath.

"Why the hell would I overreact?" Mark asked.

"Because you are already overreacting. You are like Mr. Macho Man on alpha-steroids with your attitude, and I need to explain so I need you to take a deep breath and goos-frab-a that shit down. Rub your ears like they showed in the movie Anger Management if it helps."

"Kate," I heard Mark growl and knew he was ready to blow the control on his anger. I took a deep breath myself and slowly turned to look at him.

"Mark, I believe you remember my best friend," Kate lost her attitude and spoke softly as the intensity of the moment grew.

At first glance he was exactly the same. He was so handsome, almost dream-like standing there in front of me just like he had been the day he brought me the case file in his favorite white button down with the cuffs rolled up to show off his tattoo.

His blue jeans and black boots with the matching belt that held his gun and detectives badge. His brown hair that was styled to perfection and parted on the side made me want to run my fingers through it. His blue eyes that could tear into my soul and brand me with just one glance were now staring at me in disbelief.

"What the fuck?" Mark gritted through his teeth as he glanced over me for the third time. "Are you – no fucking way," The vein above his furrowed brows throbbed violently as it commonly did when he was really angry. "Where the fuck have you been?"

I stood speechlessly as Mark reached up and lifted my hair to look at it and pushed my hair away from my shoulders. "How the fuck?" He asked as he picked up the noose-necklace from around my neck and stared at it. Then he dropped it down and I bit my lip as his fingers brushed my skin. "Why?" He asked, but I had no words for him as the anger seemed to be winning the battle with him.

"You died," he replied and I turned to walk away. He grabbed my elbow and my nerve endings came to life as electricity pulsed through me at his touch. "You left us," Mark replied as he let out a sigh. He was finally coming down from the anger as a tear fell from my eye.

"Brooklyn?" Mark asked as he looked me over from head to toe again. Only my hair and skin had changed, but everyone seemed to be looking at all of me. As if I wasn't me anymore, and maybe I wasn't but physically they should not see that. I watched him take a deep breath and run his hand through his hair as he did whenever he didn't know what to do.

I stood there and waited for the yelling or screaming or whatever it was that he wanted to throw my way, but finally nothing but silence came.

I was in another world as the traffic was silenced, and the smell of coffee and hot dogs from the sidewalk carts evaporated. The only thing I knew was Mark. I could feel him without his touch. I could smell his sandalwood scent that often set my heart into overdrive. I could hear his breaths stumble as he pushed through the emotional wave he had just been dealt. Biting my lip, a little harder as he pushed the edge of my shirt and glanced at my new tattoo I tasted blood. Finally when Mark called my name for the last time, all I could see was him, and those blues eyes I wanted to drown in. "Brook?"

"Mark," I replied with a quivering lip. He grabbed me and pulled me up against his chest and broke the hold I had on my tears. One year I lived in fear that he was dead. Three hundred sixty-five days I dreamt of being in his arms. Every day I loved him. Every second of agony from that time away from him was worth it to be in his arms right now. I laid my head on his chest while he held me tight and listened to the rapid beats of the golden heart that took a bullet for me. We stood there while the people all around us passed us by. In our own little world where nothing could get to us, until his girlfriend's voice broke the moment.

"Hey, honey, who is this?" Maya asked as she came up on us, and Mark let me go.

"This is," Mark's voice froze and I noticed his red-rimmed eyes. I wiped the tears from mine and took a deep breath as I stepped back. Seemed like the alpha in Mark was either in shock or stunned and needed a minute so I decided I would speak.

"Hi, I am Brooklyn Montgomery. I am working with District Attorney Taylor Cross here in New York County and Mark's, umm," my eyes flashed to Mark, who was still staring at me as though he had seen a ghost. "Well, I knew Mark a long time ago," I took a step closer and held out my hand for her to shake. She looked at my hand and then speechlessly stared at me as her face went from something resembling shock to pure disgust.

"I thought you said this bitch was dead," Maya declared to Mark. I thought maybe I was hearing things, but Maya placed herself between Mark and myself taking her stance. I clenched my fists as anger flooded my veins. I was doing my bank account in my head to see if I had bail money, but before I could throw a punch, Kate crossed my path and got in Maya's face.

"My friend literally just came back from the dead how about showing a little respect," Kate spoke loudly and I wanted to stay angry, but paranoia was taking over as eyes were staring at us.

"She only came back to take what is mine!" Maya yelled back as she pointed her finger, and the crowd focused all eyes on me. *Don't freak out, don't freak out – too late I was freaking out.*

"If you have trouble holding onto your man that is something you need to fix in your relationship!" Kate screamed as she placed her hands on Maya and gave her a little push to force her back and out of her face.

"It is hard to keep a man when someone like her had an NYPD blue carpet rolled up to her vagina for them to all climb inside."

As much as I wanted to punch Maya I had to get the hell out of there. They were attracting too much attention. My racing heart was already half way through a marathon before I could catch my next breath. RJ could be anywhere, and I could wind up filleted on his knife or the press might get called, and I didn't know how to explain my return. I was starting to panic as the crowd encircled us as Maya pushed Kate back.

I looked to Mark, but he had that I-have-girls-fighting-over-me look on his face as Kate bellowed again.

"Maybe Mark won't succumb to the temptation if you spread your legs or if you dropped to your knees and opened your mouth once in a while."

That was it, they were going to fight and I had to go. I pushed through the crowd that was surrounding us and then walked as fast as I could away. I broke into a sprint when I heard Mark call my name loudly.

"Brooklyn, wait," Mark shouted as I picked up speed. I rounded the corner without looking and ran into someone. My body fell to the ground and I scrambled to see who it was.

I looked up to see RJ as the sun pierced down into my eyes.

Chapter Eight

I tried to crawl away and get back on my feet when I felt a hand and began swinging and kicking. Suddenly, the helping hands let go of me. I got to my feet and pulled my weapon to see it was Derrick instead. *Was I going insane?*

"Brook, put the gun down," Derrick spoke softly with his hands up and I tried to calm my laboured breathing and racing heart as sweat broke out across my brow. I looked back to see Mark breaking up the fight and took a deep breath.

I dropped my arms but scanned my surroundings twice before I put the gun back in its holster. My skin flared as my body was not ready to let go of the anxious paranoia that was enveloping me. RJ had to be somewhere nearby waiting and watching. *He always was before.*

"What are you doing here?" I asked as he took my hand in his as if to say everything was okay. My heart was throbbing in my ears from the fear I couldn't shake. I needed to make peace with what was coming and be better prepared for when RJ did show his face.

"Heard there was a chick fight and didn't want to miss it," he replied with a smile.

"What are you really doing here?" I asked and his face fell.

"We got the DNA report back from the finger," Derrick held my hand and no more words needed to be said. I knew it was my dad's finger. "The finger was on ice for a long time but was removed before he was killed. I am sorry, Brooklyn."

"Its fine," I lied. "RJ will probably use his body parts to torture me, but I won't let it get to me because my dad is in a better place. My dad feels no pain."

Derrick pulled me into his arms and I embraced his warmth. The exhaustion from Taylor's questions, and the agony of seeing Mark's flavor of the week, and then confirming that was my dad's finger had me ready to crawl into a bed with a gallon of wine flavored ice cream and stay there for a month. I needed a friend I could trust right now and Derrick was being one.

"Brook wait!" Mark yelled as he came jogging near with Kate and Maya in tow. Derrick didn't let me go until the girls started arguing again and they were closing in on us.

"Katie you are such a bitch. Take your whore friend and go home. Stay away from my Mark," Maya bellowed as she tried to stop her lip from bleeding with her torn shirt.

"Maya, I will only say this once. My fucking name is Kate. K-A-T-E not Katie. Second, if I were you I would close my mouth before I shut it permanently and you're eating your dinners through a tube in your stomach," Kate responded as she brushed her hair with her fingers looking as though she wasn't just fighting.

"No one likes a skank who can spell," Maya replied in response to Kate spelling her name. It was one of the weakest comebacks I had ever heard. "Stay away from Mark and his penis," she screamed at me.

"Why? Brooklyn had his lollipop before you did," Kate spoke sarcastically and then gave me a wink as they came closer. "You should watch what you say about the girl who taught your man how to eat pussy. You should be getting Brooklyn a thank you present instead of name calling."

"Kate," Mark growled and I realized it was never going to end. Kate obviously didn't like Maya and neither did I, but she was using my return to say whatever she thought.

"I know, Maya, it is really hard to follow behind Brooklyn in bed because she could suck start a Harley blindfolded with her arms tied behind her back with the flu," Kate continued ignoring Mark's warning.

"Do me the biggest favor I could ask for and kiss me. It will end the cat fight. Maya will think I am with you and I need that right now," I whispered to Derrick.

He looked at Mark slowly coming at us and the two girls still arguing. They started pushing each other again as they followed him. Derrick nodded his head and then wrapped one hand around the back of my neck and brushed my cheek with his thumb. I saw Mark stop walking and even let go of Kate and Maya as he stared when I put my hands on Derrick's waist.

Derrick leaned in for the kiss that was supposed to stop an argument from attracting attention but instead was attracting attention all on its own.

His lips molded to mine as I welcomed him to kiss me harder. I moaned a little when his tongue grazed my lips and I opened for him. The flavor rush of cinnamon invaded my pores. Fire flamed under my skin, and my clit pulsed with my heart. It had been a year since

I had been kissed like this and I was going to enjoy the hell out of this one.

His tongue grazed mine as I pulled on his shirt to bring him closer. He released my neck to grab my blond hair and moved me to fit him while resting his other hand near my waist. Added heat flooded my veins with the knowledge that Mark was watching. *What was it with me and men in the protection services?*

By the time Mark called my name the second time I was breathless, and turned on. *Who knew this guy could kiss like that?*

"Hi Marshal Stevens," Kate called out sarcastically so that Mark would know who he was. I turned and looked at Mark, who was oblivious to the fact that Maya was hanging on him. He stared at me as though he was in shock once more.

"This is Derrick Stevens he, umm," I had to catch my breath after that kiss. Derrick placed a hand on the small of my back as my blood continued to race with each brush of his hand. "He was my Marshal," I muttered under my breath.

Derrick held out his free hand and met everyone. After shaking Mark and Maya's hands, I pulled his hand off the small of my back and curled into him so his arm was around me the whole time. He was minimal comfort in what felt like could become an explosive conversation.

"Marshal? As in witness protection? What do you mean he *was*?" Mark asked and I stayed silent. As with Taylor, it was best to just sit there and wait for all the questions before trying to answer one. "Does that mean you're safe now that you are home? Does this mean RJ has been caught? Is he dead? Why wasn't the NYPD notified?"

"Detective Stone isn't it?" Derrick asked and Mark nodded his head as he narrowed his eyes at Derrick. They seemed to be doing the-two-dogs-pissing-on-one-tree thing, but I was the tree and no one was going to act like I was their territory. I was Switzerland and I wasn't having it.

"That is my Mark- I mean that is Mark Stone," I stated hoping it would interrupt the testosterone daggers that were being thrown, but it didn't. They continued to ignore me, but Maya heard me and her estrogen arrows were pointed and ready to fire at me.

"I knew your name from the case file. Your office should have been notified that Miss Montgomery was not happy where she was and has chosen to withdraw her life from the care of the Marshal Service and that she was returning home. Her safety is still at risk as he had made contact prior to her moving back to New York, but there was no talking her out of it."

Mark took a step forward leaving Maya to pout and I wanted to grin when I saw it, but I kept my mouth still. I began to sulk as the throbbing vein in Mark's head raced and he glared at me as though I had just pissed him off in a really bad way. I have never seen him look so angry.

"Tell me if I get this straight. You got shot with all of us, but you were whisked away by the feds to be put into witness protection. You left us all to believe you died so you could live, and we could live safely. Then you decided that you had had enough so you come home and back into the dragon's lair?" I nodded my head. "Are you a suicide risk or did you selfishly want us to mourn you twice?"

I decided not to answer. Instead, I watched Mark struggled to get a hold of his anger. I don't know how I would feel if he popped up out of nowhere, but I know how I feel when I see Maya stroking his back and telling him everything will work out. *I wanted to rip her hair out.* Kate smiled at me and gave me the I-can-eff-her-up nod as if she knew what I was thinking.

"Where are you living?" Mark asked as he gritted his teeth.

"In my old apartment in Tribeca," I whispered.

"Jesus Christ woman! Did it not occur to you to try and make it a challenge for RJ to get to you? How many people have to get shot before you start using your survival instincts?" Mark stated as he clenched his fist and flexed his jaw. He looked furious. "Why not put up a big neon flashing sign above your building that says 'Murderers apply here?'"

"Mark, she is not worth all this," Maya whispered to Mark. He turned on her in an instant and looked as though she was the enemy.

"Maya, seriously! Now is not the time or place. Just leave it alone, or go home," Mark glared right through her.

"Mark," Maya spoke up, but the look he gave her had her backing down and for that one fleeting second I felt sorry for her. Even I knew not to push him when he was this upset. *You never poke the bear.*

"Does Taylor know?" Mark asked and I nodded. "What was I thinking? Of course you went to see him first."

"Mark, I-," I didn't know how to say anything as my words jumbled in my head. I was an educated, strong, capable woman until it came to Mark. Around him, I was a blubbering idiot.

"What Brooklyn? You want to tell me something else to add to my stress level. How about how was Taylor's dick when you saw him? Or how about you tell me why you are kissing your Marshal? There are fucking rules Brooklyn, and I thought someone like you would know how to follow them," He sneered and I took a step toward him as he took a step back. The constant back and forth with him before we got shot nearly drove me out of my mind was present here and now.

"I um-," I couldn't think how to string my words together to calm him down. "This isn't some coloring sheet where if I go outside the lines I have done something wrong. If I go outside the lines, it is because I am making my own art. My life, my choices, my coloring sheet!"

"Have a nice life, Brooklyn," Mark groaned as he was trying to hide his frustrations.

"I am glad to see that you are happy and alive," I spoke softly because in the route we were headed everyone was going to go home with a black eye or bloody lip because I was stressed out with everything that had happened since we landed in New York.

"Brooklyn do you even have a phone number?" He asked with a sigh as if he was trying to let go of the fury. I pulled out the receipt from my jeans pocket where we purchased the phone. It had the phone number written at the top. I watched as he folded it and placed it in his pocket. As he and Maya turned to walk away, I finally found my stress relieving words.

"I am so sorry that you got shot because of me. I must have told you a dozen times while they had you on the respirator, but I didn't know if you heard me." I sighed as my brain showed me the video feed of Mark breathing through a tube down his throat as the heart monitor went beep-beep in the background. I had to get this out to get any peace or hope of moving past him.

"Mark I don't know when I will have another opportunity so I just wanted to be able to express to you how sorry I am about everything that happened that day."

Maya's phone rang and Mark looked over at her as she turned her back to answer it. Then he stepped toward me.

"You were at the hospital?" Mark asked as he crossed his arms and looked over at

Derrick. While I wiped the tears from my eyes. Being near him was emotional overload, and to see him with her just made it worse.

"Of course I was there Mark. I loved you. I wanted to help get you better." I whispered so Maya wouldn't hear.

"We literally had to use force to remove her from your room to get her into protective custody. She has asked about you every day," Derrick answered and another tear rolled down my cheek as I remembered trying to stay. I had gripped the doorframe and screamed at Mark to wake up for me, as they had come in with a court order and carted me away to safety.

"She gave two Marshals a black eye and broke one's wrist trying to stay with you, but we had an order to remove her immediately."

Derrick took the small step up behind me and put his hands on my waist as the crowds thickened around us. It was lunch time and there was about to be a rush of people trying to get their food and head back to work. I knew Derrick was uneasy with me out in a crowd and so was I.

Mark's eyes drifted down to Derrick's hands and he seemed to be working something out in his head.

"I see that you are in capable hands to keep you satisfied – I mean alive, but I want my men around you. Last I heard there was still a reward for RJ so do not confront him just call us. I will see what we can do to get a security detail on you, but for now I will send Abbott and Costello. Now, where are you headed?"

The way he said the word *satisfied* echoed in my head. I went from heartbroken to pissed to scared and anxious to sad and then I was livid. Nothing about any of this day was going as I pictured it in my head.

"Satisfied?" I looked at him and rolled my eyes. "I am headed to the salon. I was thinking of dying my hair NYPD blue. After all, I should try and match the carpet rolled up to my vagina."

Chapter Nine

Kate and I spent the morning getting our makeovers and Derrick and I made plans for dinner since he didn't know anyone here.

I walked into the bar inside the Marriott Marquis. My black heels clicked on the marble floor as I made my way over to the burgundy colored chairs where Derrick was waiting for me.

When he saw me, he stood up and gave me a kiss on the cheek and held his hand out for me to sit with him.

"You are acting like a gentleman," I spoke softly.

"Yea," he stated and smiled at me.

"I see we are back to the one-word answers," I laughed.

"What?" Derrick asked and we both laughed that he had done it again.

"You always seem to love one word responses. It has been that way since I met you," I smiled as a waitress brought us two long island ice teas.

"I didn't realize I did that." Derrick lifted his glass. "To your new life, and all that it will entail."

"Actually it kind of sucks," I murmured and took a drink of my drink.

"Change your mind about coming back with me. We can move you and set up some kind of note delivering system. I can hide you from him."

"I do trust you to keep me safe. It is not that. Life just isn't what I expected," I whispered.

"What did you expect?" Derrick asked and I thought about it. I had expected a fairy tale, even though I knew that it was merely fiction.

"I just need to find a way to be myself again. I was fun, adventurous, a little quirky, but most of all I was happy being me. I don't feel that way now, and I never expected anyone to show anger at my return and Mark was pissed."

"Then you need to start doing whatever it takes to make yourself happy. What were you doing before that you are not doing now?" Derrick waited, but I had no answer. For me, life stood still, frozen in time. While everyone else moved on with their lives and found a way to live without me, I only survived by thinking about them. I never moved on.

"I need to wrap myself up in a case, get laid, get drunk, and when it is safer, I need to sneak around my security."

"Come on," Derrick whispered and stood up. He waved over at Abbott and Costello, who I forgot about because I was so used to being followed anyway.

"What are we doing?" I asked with a giggle when I saw the mischief on his face. "Where are we going?"

"Montgomery, show me what you got. You are perfectly safe with me so show me how to sneak around your security."

With laughter, I grabbed his hand and we took off running towards the elevator. After some quick and lucky timing, I was able to wave to Costello before the doors shut and we moved up floor after floor.

"Press the 4th from the top," I spoke in a rush as I pulled my shoes off. "Give me a boost." Derrick cupped his hand and helped me up as I lifted the paneling in the elevator.

When I got on top of the elevator, I took my shoes and then reached in for Derrick. He was heavy but with help from the golden bar along the wall he was able to pull himself up onto the roof.

"Now what Montgomery?" He asked and I nearly burst out with laughter as I closed the paneling.

"Patience," I warned. There in the dark we rode up to the 45th floor and then returned back down to the lobby. Somewhere along the way we picked up Abbott on his phone.

"Here we go again," Abbott yelled into his phone. I covered my mouth so they would not hear the laughter as Derrick tickled my sides. "I don't care what her tracker says she is not in this elevator."

Abbott got off the elevator somewhere around the 20th floor to help Costello look for me. Once more Derrick and I were alone again in the dark.

"Thank you for coming with me. This is the most fun I have had in a long time." I spoke softly.

"Montgomery, there is something addictive about you. I should be in Tennessee right now, but instead I am here watching over you because there is something magnetic about you."

"They have AA meetings for people who meet me," I laughed, but my smile fell as Derrick put his fingers under my chin to raise my eyes to his. Riding on top of the elevator

Derrick leaned forward and placed his lips on mine.

As I opened to his cinnamon flavor, I got a rush of heat charging through me. His thin silky lips made me want to kiss him all day. He pulled me down into his lap and held me there against him. I felt safe and warm as he pressed his lips back against mine.

"I have to leave tomorrow, but can I see you again?" Derrick asked when he breathlessly pulled away.

"We'll see. I sort of have a date tonight with Kate," I spoke softly. "It is a girl's night, but I have a few hours between now and then."

"Do you want to come back to my room?"

"I don't know," I replied nervously. I didn't know what I wanted and didn't want to make a decision I would regret with all the sudden changes that were happening.

Derrick placed a softened kiss on my neck, and I ran my fingers through his brown hair. He wasn't Mark, but he knew how to light the fire inside me to make my flesh crawl with the need for his touch.

"Derrick," I whispered in the dark, and he pulled back and looked at me. "I don't have my heart back yet."

"Brooklyn, I don't want your heart," Derrick sighed. "At least not until you let go of the man you have been holding onto since I met you."

"He's my Mark," I whispered into the dark as Derrick pulled me tighter to him.

"Brooklyn he is not your Mark anymore. Those people you came back for all moved on without you and have changed. He looked at Maya with love and concern. I saw what your eyes are avoiding, I saw how he feels about her. I don't want to see you get hurt while you cling to the history you two used to have."

"Want to see the roof?" I asked climbing off of Derrick and holding onto the cables as the elevator continued to move. I refused to acknowledge what he said because I wasn't ready to hear or accept it.

"Show me your escaping skills, Montgomery," Derrick replied and I laughed. I was so glad I had Derrick. He could be fun when he wanted to be.

Kate decided we needed to have a girl's night of karaoke. I sang, danced, and drank through the night. It was awesome to be out with her like no time had gone by. It had taken me a while to warm up to being out in public, but the liquid courage in my cup kept my belly warm and my paranoia down.

The darkened club illuminated my white halter dress under the black lights. I had borrowed the dress from Kate as I had lost weight over the last year and nothing fit quite right. I was a little shorter than her so the dress flowed down to my knees. I still had my gun on, but thankfully this dress didn't show the outline of it as it sat on my upper thigh.

"Brooklyn," Kate yelled over the music and pointed across the room for me to see Mark standing there looking as delicious as always. He was dressed in a black button down with the sleeves rolled up and a pair of jeans that sported his badge. *Wonder what he wanted.*

I got a new drink and walked over to him. I thought maybe I had had too much to drink, but I shoved the thought aside when my mind starting thinking about all the things I wanted to do to this man. When I could picture handcuffs and whips I knew it was official I was drunk. Sober that stuff scared the hell out of me.

"Hi," I shouted above the music. "Did you come out to sing for me?" I asked trying to be friendly as I sipped the long island iced tea from the straw in the glass. Our last conversation ended in turmoil maybe this time it could be amicable.

"I came to talk to you," Mark whispered in my ear. He was so close to me that I could inhale his sandalwood scent and my mind flashed to the first time we had had sex. Then I wanted to cry as I thought about the earlier conversation and the last time we were together. *The day we died.*

"Well then, talk," I shouted over the music as I spun the straw in my glass. I had to focus to keep my emotions under control as the fiery warm drink in my belly took away my inhibitions.

"Come on," Mark whispered as he took my drink and sat it down. He nodded to Kate as people started coming up and saying hi to him. I guess with my death he spent a lot of time out as people I didn't know stopped to shake his hand. He took my arm and led me outside to his black Escalade that was parked in the middle of the lot.

Chapter Ten

"Get in the car Brooklyn," Mark growled and I climbed into the back seat of his Escalade.

"Why are we in the back seat?" I asked, and he shot me a look that said it was a dumb question as he climbed inside and shut his door.

"I just need a minute with you, and when someone looks for someone they typically look at the front of the car, and not the darker tinted windows in the back."

Leave it to a detective to know how to find privacy when he needed it. I took a deep breath and prepared myself for the proverbial I-am-sorry-our-conversation-sucked   followed by the I-am-with-someone speech and the I-can't-be-around-you finish. As well as more questions, as Taylor had left me   four voicemails with nothing but questions.

"Brooklyn I came tonight because I wanted to see how you were."

"I will be fine when I get my life back, and can stop looking over my shoulder all the time," I replied as I played with my hands in my lap.

"Brook, I just need to know for my own sanity are you with Derrick or Taylor?" I watched as his jaws clenched and he glared ahead at me. "Or both?"

"Does it matter?"

"I don't trust them," Mark uttered under his breath. "I promised your dad I would take care of you. I need to know that you will be safe and protected. I want to know that whoever you are with can do that. You do have a very serious psychopath gunning for you." The silence was deafening and I wanted another drink. It was uncomfortable to discuss RJ with Mark, and I couldn't figure out why.

"I need to know that you will be all right with them because you are quite the handful." Mark slid a half smile up at me and I relaxed into the seat and smiled back at him. I used to be quite the handful, but Mark hadn't been around so he didn't know how broken I really was.

"Costello called me and told me about the Marriott. Why would you ditch them your first day back?" I shrugged my shoulders. "Brooklyn I can't lose you again. Tell me one of those belligerent morons can watch over you and keep you safe. Tell me who you are with."

"I am not with either man," I took a deep breath and continued on my path of honesty and blurted out more information than what was needed. "There hasn't been anyone since you because I was living my life waiting for you."

I closed my eyes to hide my embarrassment from my inability to let go of him. I was trying, but it had been like seven hours.

I knew one day I would find the one for me, but right now it wasn't Taylor or Derrick. To be honest, it wasn't anyone until I let Mark go. This would be the hardest thing I ever had to do. Facing down a killer was nothing when losing Mark felt like I was being torn inside out and devoured.

I felt a warm rush as something touched my scar. I opened my eyes to see Mark examining it and his finger was lightly grazing the sensitive spot.

"You got shot," Mark stated as if he was putting the pieces together. "I heard that you were trapped under me and helpless to defend yourself, but yet you are still here," I nodded my head.

His finger grazed over my new tattoo that sat on my arm above my scar and investigated it. It was the shape of a heart with a sinus rhythm inside that flat lines. Just outside of the flat line were three roses leaving my heart in a dove's talons. Each of the roses carried a name written in tiny script in the leaves, but Mark's name was written at the base because he was holding on the longest.

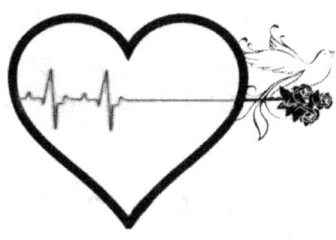

"What does this mean?" Mark asked as each graze of his finger over my flesh left a fire behind on my skin. "Is this about your dad?" He asked and I shook my head. He trailed his finger over it again and asked "Is this about you?" I shook my head. As he grazed it again, I bit my lip in hopes of keeping my words inside. "What is this about Brooklyn?"

Mark pulled me into the middle seat and took a closer look at my tattoo. When I felt his breath on my skin I wanted to groan, but instead I curled my toes and continued biting my lip. I knew he was going to see his name, but didn't want to answer as to why his name was flat-lined near my heart.

"Brooklyn you are going to make your lip bleed. Now stop and talk to me."

"Where is your girlfriend tonight?" I asked and the glimmer in his eyes said at this moment he didn't care.

"Maya is where she needs to be at the moment, and that is anywhere but here," I went to speak, but Mark held his finger up to my lips and continued on.

"Abbott and Costello know you are here with me, and they are fine with it. They know I am not here to hurt you. Now tell me what the new tattoo means. I thought after we got your butterfly before law school you said you would never get another."

"I wanted an emblem to mark the day on my body."

"What day, Brooklyn?" Mark asked as he pulled back. I needed him to stay close to me and allow me to stay drunk off the pull he had to me.

"It is the day we died," I whispered under my breath.

"You didn't die Brooklyn," Mark stated and I could see the confusion written on his face.

"We died Mark," I took a deep breath and allowed him to study it further. I felt his finger slide over his name and wanted to cry out. I wanted him to leave Maya. I wanted my heart to be whole. I wanted to erase the last eighteen months and never take the job with Taylor. I just wanted Mark.

"I hurt you so bad because I thought I could change what was going to happen before it happened. Then you got shot and I watched you die on me," tears start falling as I am trying to explain. "The tattoo represents our death as a couple, as friends, and as people."

I had had way too much to drink to keep my emotions bottled and my mouth closed.

"The roses represent the good in my life leaving. The dove represents you all moving on and finding peace without me. The heart flat lining is from the moment you saw me in Taylor's lap and from when I saw you and Kate get shot."

"Why would you brand yourself such a painful memory?" Mark asked as he opened Pandora's Box with his question. I blew it off with a shrug because I was speechless when my body was strumming to its own alcoholic beat under the heat of his touch. It wasn't until he stopped touching me that I could get a word out.

"Mark, I am so sorry I hurt you. You will never know how sorry I am. There are days where I can't breathe because I feel like everything that happened was my fault and I never got to tell you I was sorry. I never wanted to cause you any pain. I only wanted you. I have always wanted you. What I mean is that I have loved you since our first day in Kindergarten. Who would have known that little boy who protected me from the bullies on the playground would do it every day of his life? I know things are different now, but please know that there is not a day that goes by that I don't feel responsible, and I am so sorry to have put you through that."

I felt hands on my arms lifting me. I lifted my skirt as I straddled his lap. He wrapped his arms around me bringing me in for a hug. As I wrapped my arms around his neck. I held on tight as I cried on his shoulder.

"Brooklyn you can't carry this stuff around with you. I let it go and forgot about it."

After a few moments, I leaned back and sniffled while looking into his cobalt eyes. *He forgot about it?* I reached for the top button and began unbuttoning his black shirt.

"Brooklyn what are you doing?" He asked as he put his hands over mine to stop me. I shook his hands off and he just watched me.

When I got his shirt open, I stared at the tanned chest that rippled with hardened muscle. He looked like a magazine cover model in every way except for the crooked heart-shaped scar on his chest.

I ran my fingers over his scar and could feel his heart race with every touch. He felt about his scar and me touching it as I did when he touched mine. We were broken and we wore the evidence every day. I took his hand and placed it on my scar as I held mine over his.

"You can't forget about it. These are reminders of what I had done to us. It is a daily reminder for me of the day my life ended. It is a reminder that life is short, and to be wary of your decisions as they could be your last."

"Brooklyn, they are just scars. They will fade and that moment in time will drift away until it is a forgotten memory," Mark spoke softly as he pushed my black hair out of my face as the air thickened with the grief I felt for what happened to him.

I sniffled and a new tear escaped my eye and dropped onto his chest as I laid my forehead on his.

"I can't ever forget watching you die. Everything in me shattered in that instant, and my life ended. I wake up sweating in the night remembering pushing on you and screaming at you to live for me."

Mark pulled me down to him and placed my lips on his. I groaned when I felt his velvet tongue brush my lip asking for entry. I nearly cried when the flavor of coffee and whipped cream flooded my senses. Even though I knew it was just a kiss, it felt like I was finally home.

"Brooklyn," Mark muttered against my lips as I involuntarily ground myself into his hardening cock. My alcohol fueled body had taken control and I was merely along for the ride.

"What?" I asked as I pulled myself back and leaned forward as I placed the softest of kisses on his scar. I heard an intake of breath and felt him grab my hair as my tongue reached out to taste the ripples in his flesh.

"Fuck! Brooklyn we have to stop," Mark groaned.

"Then stop me," I murmured. "Tell me no," I replied sending him back the same words he had said to me the first night I ever let him inside me. He had already owned my heart at that point, but one magical ride on his cock and my soul was branded his.

Mark's eyes and face lit up as headlights turned into the parking lot. In that fleeting moment as the light struck us, we were Mark and Brooklyn again. We had no significant others, no responsibilities to anyone, and just relished the feel of each other. Mark took my head and pulled me down to his lips as I shuffled on his lap. Then he kissed me hard as I ground into him.

"You're wearing your gun," Mark stated breathlessly. I murmured something in the form of a yes while I pushed my body against his. "It is piercing my leg."

I pulled back and looked at the bright eyes I loved to get lost in, and uttered the words that every man should want to hear.

"Then take it off."

I watched as Mark slid his hands inside my dress and pulled the Velcro apart. Then his hand grazed that thin strip of silk covering my bare mound as he went to pull apart the top strip.

"You are soaking wet." Mark gritted through his teeth. I nodded my head as he pulled my holster off my thigh and tossed it on the seat.

"Brooklyn-," I bit down on his neck as I pushed my pelvis into his hardened cock. I heard his groan and felt his heart race as he threw his head back. "Brooklyn-," He gritted his teeth as I went to reach behind me and unclip my dress to let it fall forward.

I felt hands pull my arms down and I sat back up. I saw the pained look on his face and knew what was coming before he said those five little words.

"Brooklyn I can't do this," there they were the words I knew would come. My stomach sank, but I didn't cry as I was expecting them. "Maya is waiting for me."

I felt cold and a little embarrassed as the alcohol dissipated in my body. I climbed off Mark's lap and sat back in the seat beside him.

"Brooklyn you seem to think what we had was good. I know you love me, and I love you, but a relationship is about so much more than great sex, love, and friendship."

"What else do you need?" I asked.

"Trust," Mark replied.

I fixed my dress and waited to hear what I knew was coming. I knew there was trust broken between us, but what did he expect. Every day we went from hot to cold because he was keeping secrets. I thought I could look past it because he owned my heart, but apparently while I could ignore that rift he couldn't.

"You stopped trusting me the minute your dad and I told you everything. It is why you let Taylor into our bed that night, and it is why we would have never worked," Mark placed his finger under my chin and forced me to look at him. "You are the forbidden fruit, and I can smell how delicious you taste. I could take you, bend you over and fuck you all weekend long, but come Monday morning I would be gone and you would have a broken heart."

I climbed out of his SUV and started walking away from the building. I needed air or something. I had known this was coming, but it didn't stop the sting from his words.

"Brooklyn," Mark shouted as I heard him running behind me. I turned to see he was buttoning up his shirt as he was trying to catch up.

"Mark, please," I put my hand up to stop him. "Just turn around and walk back inside. You can tell Kate I am going home now that I am completely humiliated and horny."

"Brooklyn, don't be like that. I seriously want us to be friends."

"I have tasted your cock," I groaned.

"So?"

"Don't you get it? I have had the forbidden fruit and loved it and now you want me to sit by and watch as someone else has it?" I rolled my eyes. "I have endured enough torture, I won't self-inflict it by watching you be with her," I turned and walked toward the end of the parking lot. I heard footsteps behind me and felt a tug on my arm.

"Don't be like that Brooklyn. We have history Brooklyn, and because of that I can help you get off, but I am with Maya now. Tell me what to do because you were my best friend and I want to keep you that way," Mark whispered and I involuntarily groaned.

"We can't be friends Mark! I got turned on and kissed a taken man. I am no better than what your girlfriend thinks of me. You are insane if you think that we can be friends. I can't even sit in a car with you without trying to have what isn't mine."

Mark grabbed me to him and placed his soft lips on mine. I molded to him for a moment, but then I bit his lip and pushed off him.

"I miss arguing with you Brooklyn," Mark stated when I looked inquisitively at him. "Fuck -Brooklyn I miss you. You know I didn't ask for any of this. I moved on because you were dead."

As I got ready to lecture Mark, a black SUV rolled up and I turned to look at it as my heart raced. My body trembled with anxiety as the window slowly rolled down Mark stood in front of me. Once again ready to take a bullet for me.

"Devochka Moya, come get in the car and I will take you home." I stared at the face that matched my father's as my uncle Anton called out for me in his pet name that meant I was his little angel.

"What are you doing here?" I asked as I hadn't seen him since I had pigtails and played in parks.

"I am watching over an angel because I promised my brother I would protect her."

"Have you been following me?" I asked and Anton gave me the look that said my father's men were all around me. I spun around taking in the view of the parking lot and saw at least five cars full of my father's men. I suddenly realized that I wasn't as on-guard as I needed to be because I hadn't even noticed.

I took a few steps forward and turned to look at Mark.

"Mark, I love you. You hung the moon and the stars for me. I needed to come back and end us. You and I needed to be canceled like a bad tv sitcom, where people would say remember when, but no one really does." I placed my hand over his scar before he could button the top buttons and leaned up to place a kiss on his cheek. "I needed to hear you say it was over. I needed the goodbye."

I turned to walk away when Mark caught my arm and I looked back at the questions on his face. I put up one finger to Anton and turned back to Mark.

"Brooklyn we have been over for a year; why would you need to hear that?"

"Because my life was frozen in time. Living in the fantasy world of witness protection coming home to you is what got me through each day. I needed the closure so maybe I could move on."

"But you didn't know if I was alive," Mark stated as if challenging my reasoning.

"In my mind, you were alive and you were hunting to find me, to protect me, to love me. I took the old photo we had in the seashell frame with me when I left. You were the first thing I saw when I woke up and the last thing I kissed when I went to bed. I prayed that you would find me every single day. When I had

had enough waiting. When I had had my fill of wondering how you were. I came home instead of waiting for you to find me."

"Brooklyn I-," I put up my hand and cut him off.

"Mark I am eternally grateful to you for all that you did for me, and that when my life ended, it ended with you by my side. I told you if I only had one more night to live, I wanted it to be with you and that is what I got. All I ever wanted was for my life to begin and end with you."

"Brooklyn, I didn't come for you because we all thought you died."

"I did die Mark. I am not Brooklyn anymore."

Then I was finally able to walk away without him stopping me.

Chapter Eleven

"Anton why do you have men following me?" I asked as he sped toward my apartment.

"Your father made me promise to look after you and they all wanted to. Most of those men watched you grow up, Devochka Moya, my angel. They want to save you from the evil that killed your father," Anton spoke with such a thick Russian accent that he reminded me of my dad, and it made my heart hurt.

"You guys have to stop following me," I demanded, but I could see from the look on Anton's face that I would never be alone again. I thought coming home I would have freedom, but instead it was like it was with the Marshal's. I was always under someone's microscope.

My phone began to ring and I pulled it from the pocket of my dress.

"Hello."

"Montgomery," Derrick responded.

"Hi," I replied and a smile. "What are you doing?"

"Checking on you," he replied and when I said nothing he kept talking. "I had this feeling that you were in need of someone to make you smile."

"Why would you feel that way?" I asked looking over at Anton as he tried his best to figure out who I was talking to.

"I don't know. It was just something my gut told me and I always go with what my instincts tell me."

I half smiled with warmth from his caring, but my gut was telling me the timing of it all was a little coincidental.

"I am heading to the airport soon, and just wanted you to know that no matter what is happening in your life that I am thinking about you and as long as you are on my mind you are never alone. If you ever need me, I am only a phone call away."

"That is really sweet Derrick," I replied and then we soon said our goodbyes.

Upon arrival at my apartment, I turned on my television and kicked off my shoes. I went into the kitchen and poured a glass of wine. I sat on the couch and started watching the news. By the end of the viewing, there was a knock on the door.

I went to the door and opened it to see Mark standing outside my door. I opened my door further to let him in so the two cops that took over for Abbott and Costello's break wouldn't hear our conversation.

"What are you doing here?" I asked softly as I closed the door.

"We were not done talking," Mark replied.

"I don't know what else you want me to say."

I walked over to the island where I poured another glass of wine as Mark walked up behind me. He pressed his body up against mine and leaned down to next to my ear.

"We have been here before," he whispered and he was right. A year ago this is how it started before Taylor walked through the door, but things were different. I set my wine glass down and turned around to face Mark.

"It is a lot different now," I spoke softly. Mark picked me up and set me on the island. "Seeing you with her breaks my heart," I whisper as Mark pushed my hair back behind my shoulders and puts his hand under my chin to force my face up to his.

"You know I love you Brooklyn," Mark whispered as his lips came closer to mine.

"I know you love Maya," I spoke nearly silent. Mark pulled back and looked at me.

"Brooklyn what did she do?" Mark asked, but I didn't understand and twisted my mouth to the side and furrowed my brows in confusion. "When you died so did I. I was left a broken man, and Maya came in and taped the pieces of me back together. I gave her my heart because you were gone. I do love you Brooklyn and I love her, but she hasn't done anything to warrant me to leave her. She saved me when you left."

"What did I do Mark?" I asked and Mark took a step away from me. "I spent my entire life waiting for you to choose me, to pick me, to love me. I finally earned your love, but I have never been your top choice or your first pick."

"I'm sorry Brooklyn. I knew how you felt about me a year ago when you told me. I had known for a long time, but I knew if we crossed that line you would walk away the minute it didn't work."

"You mean like I did tonight?" I asked and Mark nodded. "Then there is nothing more to say. You know I want you, but can't have you, and it is unhealthy for me to try and hold on to you, so I think you should go. Don't call and don't come by. Just forget me."

There was the end of us as Brooklyn and Mark. My eyes filled with tears, and I turned my head so he wouldn't see how it affected me, but he pulled my face back to look at him.

"Brooklyn don't cry over me. I am not worth your tears," Mark spoke softly, but the tears fell anyway. I was shattered like a broken piece of glass. No matter how you tried to glue me back together, I would always be cracked and chipped.

The thought of him kept me alive, it kept me going, but now the thought of him made me want to crawl into a darkened hole and stay there till the sun burned out and life ceased to exist.

"I said goodbye. This is the part where you say it and we go our separate ways," I climbed off the island to walk away from him.

"Brooklyn she merely has my heart while you are in my soul," Mark whispered as the shadows of grief crossed his face.

"It is not enough," I mouthed the words as I turned to go into the bathroom and turn on the shower. I knew he was going to leave, but I couldn't watch him go. I stripped all my clothes off and climbed in as the first hard burst of tears knocked me to my knees.

I had loved the man for twenty years, and while I could take a lot of the blame, the final nail in the coffin of our relationship was RJ. How many men would understand being stalked by a serial killer? *None!* I would live my life empty and alone because of him. God help RJ when I found my spine and put my life back because I wouldn't stop until he had suffered like I have.

"Brook," Mark called out as my shower door opened. He walked inside completely clothed and picked me up off the floor. "You can't hide in here in hopes I will just go away." I didn't want Mark here because he was the source of my pain, but I wanted him to stay and comfort me. I was a walking contradiction. "I am not leaving you in pain like this. Hell, Brooklyn you just came back to life. Please just let me hold you for a while."

Mark held me up in the shower until my tears started to slow and the water began to chill. I reached over and cut off the water as we stood their vulnerable and broken hearted. Mark helped me step out of the shower and grabbed a towel. I wrapped it around my body and walked over to one of the boxes I had yet to unpack and pulled out my robe.

"You might want to let me put those clothes in the dryer," I spoke with a rasp from the crying. I then walked into my bedroom to allow him to change.

When he stepped out, he was wearing a white terry cloth robe holding his clothes as he headed for the dryer. I was stuck with Mark for at least an hour while his clothes dried. I pushed my door closed as I dropped my towel and went to grab my underwear from the dresser when I turned and saw Mark in my doorway holding my door open.

"You are beautiful," Mark stated as he looked over me. "You are really skinny, but you are still beautiful."

"Mark-," I started, but he came into my room and closed the door. That same pull he always had to me was as strong as ever, and I wanted to have him as my own for one minute or one second, but I knew it would only hurt me. "Mark you are not a cheater," I whispered.

"You are right, I am not," Mark stated and then tilted his head as his blue eyes memorized every inch of me. "Why does it feel like we have unfinished business?" Mark asked and I couldn't answer him because I had felt that way for a year.

I walked over to him and stuck my hand inside the robe where his scar was.

"I think destiny wanted us to die together and still being here leaves us yearning for more."

I watched as Mark untied the robe and let it fall. I raked in his body with my eyes. The man had beefed up even more since last year. I didn't think there was an ounce of fat on him, and the V on his waist forced me to look down to see he was hardening for me.

I took a step back as he came toward me. I knew that predatory glare in his eyes. He wanted to do something that he would later regret and as much as I wanted to be the voice of reason I couldn't because I was drooling just looking at him.

"Do you yearn for me?" Mark asked bringing up what I had said.

"Yes," I whispered as my back hit the wall. Mark pressed his body next to mine

"I need to have you Brooklyn. I have to taste you," Mark confessed and my heart rate leapt as my hormones celebrated.

"You are not a cheater Mark, and we both know when you leave we are done," I whispered with very little meaning behind my words.

"Maybe this is how we need to say goodbye," Mark whispered as he placed a kiss on my neck. "I am going to tell her. Do you want me to tell her now before I make you scream or would you like to scream before I tell her?" Mark asked as I felt his cock press into my belly and moisture coated my thighs.

His hands moved up and down the sides of my body as he waited for an answer. While my brain tried to distinguish between right and wrong his fingers found the little bundle of nerves between my thighs and lightly stroked them until I was panting.

"After, definitely after," I whispered and then his mouth was on me. His velvety, hot lips pressed against mine in a rush as I threaded my fingers through his hair. I felt Mark's hands on my hips as his tongue brushed my lip for entry.

When I opened, his tongue thrust against mine bringing a burst of flavor that had me moaning into his mouth. I would never get enough of the coffee and whipped cream flavor that came from Mark. The instant fire he brought into his kiss left me dizzy and breathless. I felt faint and my legs went weak, but Mark held me up as I moaned into his mouth.

My skin flamed as my blood started to boil with the need to have him. I lifted my leg to wrap around his waist trying to get friction as my clit pulsated to a rhythm that matched my heart.

Mark pushed his hardened length against my clit a few times, but his smirk said he was nowhere near ready to give me what I wanted.

He dropped his head and sucked one pink nipple into his mouth and I reached for his hair. My back bowed as my nipples hardened and my body flushed in strawberry patches to show my arousal. Then his wants outweighed my needs as I was ready to drag him back up to me and impale myself on him, but instead he leaned back and smiled as I watched his tongue reach out and lick my hardened nipple. It was intoxicating watching him watch me.

He was a fantasy I had dreamt about for a year and here he was doing everything I wanted him to without asking. In the deepest part of my core, I knew it was wrong, and we were hurting Maya, but when I stared into his eyes, I just didn't care. She had loved him for twenty minutes while I loved him for twenty years.

"Tell me what you want," Mark growled as his tongue went back and swirled my nipple before sucking it back into his mouth. My body bowed away from the wall once more trying to force him to take more, and do more.

"You, Mark. I just want you," I groaned as he lightly bit down on my nipple and then moved to suck the next one into his mouth. He continued his assault on my senses until I was gasping with need and clawing at him.

I watched as Mark dropped to his knees and lifted one leg to hang over his shoulder. I was spread open and my mound was aimed at his face. I took a deep breath and looked for something to grip as his mouth moved closer and closer.

"I always loved the way you tasted. Like the perfect spring peach, you weren't quite ready to drop from the tree until I put my hands on you, and with a little coaxing you were plucked just in time to be the sweetest and juiciest."

I bit my lip and held back a groan while his words basted me in heat. This wasn't me I didn't break the rules and destroy relationships, but with Mark's mouth at my mound and his words in my ears he made me feel really good about doing something very bad.

I watched as he took the first lick and nearly screamed as a thrill burst through my veins. I should have stopped him and saved him from making a mistake, but as my clit swelled and my protests were silenced.

Those strawberry patches now flushed nearly every inch of my skin as goosebumps flooded me. He placed one finger inside me as I grabbed my breasts to hold onto. He found that rough patch that had me forgetting my own name as he simultaneously sucked me into his mouth and licked that bundle of nerves perfectly.

"You are delicious," Mark whispered as I watched him lick his lips. I was going to combust just from looking at him. I was so close to the edge that just one more touch would send me over the edge. I pushed my pelvis into him, but he merely smiled.

"You can't come yet," he whispered as he stood up and placed his lips on mine to flood me with his flavor mixed with mine. I wrapped my arms around his neck and pulled his body to sandwich myself between him and the wall. He pulled away with a smirk.

"I am not nearly done with you," Mark growled as he picked me up and spread my legs around his waist. I felt the cold wall at my back as his cock sat at my entrance. I dug my nails into his skin as he slowly pushed through resistant flesh that hadn't been breached in a year.

"You are so tight," Mark growled as I wiggled and danced my hips on him trying to get him to shove himself inside me all at once, but he took his time making me swell to feel every nerve and vein.

"Fuck, you are killing me," Mark gritted through his teeth as sweat broke out across his brow. I saw him struggle with his self-control. I could feel his cock pulsing to his heartbeat as he filled me to the hilt.

"You okay?" Mark asked as he stayed completely still. I nodded as my eyes filled with tears as this really was a fantasy come true. I had come back from the dead and was now in his arms. I knew it wouldn't last, but it didn't stop me from admiring the moment.

"Mark," I ground out as he started to move in and out of me so very slowly. "I love you."

Mark paused and took one hand to move the hair out of my face so he could see me as sweat lined my brow, and my body trembled with the need to explode in his arms.

After staring into my eyes, something changed and he pulled me off the wall and carried me over to the bed, laying me down in the middle and climbing over me.

"Brooklyn, I do love you. You will always have the piece of my heart I gave you all those years ago," Mark whispered and I pulled his face down to mine so his lips grazed mine. Then Mark pulled back and stared into my eyes with his beautiful cobalt eyes that spoke volumes of love and loss when it came to me.

"I need," I whimpered until he started pushing his throbbing length in and out of me again.

My body strummed to the beat of Mark's movements as my pussy walls vibrated their excitement that he was deep inside me. That rough patch behind my vagina came to life as his cock grazed it in slow, methodical movements.

My hips undulated under Mark as he took my hands in his interlocking our fingers and placing them above my head. I met him thrust for thrust as my body flared with need. The way his eyes showed the love and loss he felt from me had a tear streaming out of my eyes.

"Brooklyn," Mark called my name when I tried to look away as it was getting too intense. My heart and soul were cut open and bleeding. I no longer had any resistance or barriers between my heart and Mark.

"I'm scared," I whispered and Mark halted his movements leaving my hormones to rage around his length as my body shuttered with the need for him to move.

"I won't let anything happen to you Brooklyn," Mark whispered as he kissed my tear away.

I pushed my hips up and thrust my body onto his length from underneath Mark. He caught on that I was done talking and pushed into each thrust. Within seconds, my body revved back to life as my breasts grew heavy, and my nipples hardened as they brushed against his chest.

My thighs tightened as electricity sparked in my veins and my heart pulsed through my deepest recesses. I clamped down on Mark to hear a moan that matched mine. Mark let go of my hands and pushed my knees up over his shoulders as he slammed into me over and over again.

"Fuck," I screamed as he swelled so large I could feel him everywhere. I could taste him in my throat with each thrust into me. He leaned over and bit down on my neck. I held his head there until I was sure I would be sporting a hickey.

My toes curled as he rubbed that spot he knew so well and my body broke out in renewed goosebumps as sweat broke out across my body. I tried to stop it I tried to hold back, but Mark knew my body too well.

"Let go, I will be here to catch you," Mark whispered as his breath flowed into my ear and my body reverberated with the permission he had given me.

He pushed into me a few more times and I was lost in the moment. A blaze started in my belly and sharply spread out leaving me chanting Mark's name as I lost my breath with the next wave he pushed into me. The orgasm had stolen my heart while leaving me in a blissful euphoria.

I locked eyes with Mark and watched as he pushed into me finding his own release. Then I reached up and placed my hands around the back of his neck pulling him down to lay his forehead on mine.

Mark was right about one thing he could fuck with the best of them, but he was gone before morning and he had taken a piece of me with him. I was never going to be the same.

Chapter Twelve

"Hello," I answered my phone and it was Taylor on the other end.

"Good morning sunshine," he started and then I heard him say something to his assistant. "It has been a whole month since you came back. I want you to take the morning off, and go get yourself made over. I have texted you all the appointments I have made and Kate is waiting to go with you."

I was confused, as I looked at the incoming text.

"You made me a spa appointment?" I asked because this crossed that boss-employee line. I would never forget Taylor being inside me, but I felt as though that one fleeting moment was hindering the respect he gave me at work.

I did need a day off. I had been working around the clock to handle some domestic violence cases because they had been waiting for someone to speak up for the victims. I had been strictly going from home to work and back. I made it easy on Abbott and Costello who were still tagging along.

Derrick was flying back and forth between his job in Tennessee and New York. He said he was uncomfortable with my choice, but wouldn't think of trying to talk me out of it. I was really starting to enjoy his friendship like I had with Mark. He was easy to be myself around and without the romance it was refreshing.

"Brooklyn are you listening?" Taylor asked and I shook Derrick from my mind. "Yes I made you a spa appointment. I am taking you out," Taylor replied and I smiled. "I will pick you up tonight it is a costume party."

I took a deep breath with the thought of lots of people in costumes where I wouldn't know who was who. Even scarier I knew the ins and outs at work and at home. I would be in a strange place surrounded by hidden faces. My breathing became erratic as my chest felt tight. My emotions were all over the place as my brain scattered for a sensible thought that didn't include being skinned alive. *I was my own worst enemy now.*

"Brooklyn, it will be fine. It is a double date if you count your security detail who is already on board to come. You will be perfectly safe with me."

I agreed and hung up. I changed out of work clothes and put on a pair of white skinny jeans and a silver halter top, and headed out the door to meet Kate.

Shopping for accessories on Fifth Avenue reminded me that I was still very poor. I had a credit card Anton had given me, but I really didn't want anything from him. He would never be my dad and the sooner he stopped pretending he gave a damn about me the sooner we could put the Sunday dinner charades behind us.

"Taylor is infuriating me, but yet I couldn't imagine getting through the day without his humor."

"What did he do now?" Kate asked as I looked at earrings.

"I think there has been another body because last week he locked me out of the Cut Me Not files. Then when I tried to pull the police reports, it said I needed a supervisor's consent."

"Why don't you just walk into the police station and ask Mark to pull the reports? I mean, do you know there is a victim, or are you just being overly paranoid because they want you to leave it alone?" Kate asked while we shopped at Louis Vuitton.

I picked up a pair of sunglasses and tried them on my face. I loved designer things, but not the six-hundred-dollar price tag that was attached. Soon as I saw the price tag would bankrupt me I put them down as though they had burned me.

"I don't want it to be real to be honest. If I know it is happening again then I have to get involved, but if I don't know, if I only suspect then I can go through life in denial."

"Maybe there is no body, maybe RJ is done killing those extra people and is waiting for you to get comfortable and then bam, you never see it coming." Kate was talking with her hands, but I shook my head because there was nothing he could do now that would be unexpected.

Kate and I walked over and looked at the purses. I found a brown one that looked like it would be something Kate would like and held it up to her.

"That is cute. How much?" She asked as I held the purse up and I blurted out.

"I slept with Mark," I cringed as Kate smiled at me. I had been hiding it from everyone and needed to get it out of my system.

"Thank God. I thought it was expensive. I didn't know it was as cheap as a one night stand," She laughed as she walked over to look at the price and then scoffed at it. "Was it good? How do you feel?" She asked when she walked back over to the wall rack.

"Of course it was good no one else fits me and knows me like him, but I feel like I am a piece of shit. I became the other woman. He said he was going to tell Maya, and I guess he did because I haven't seen or heard from him since."

"Of course Mark knows you like that you guys did verbal foreplay for what fifteen years. It is just familiarity, and I am glad it was Mark who popped the cherry on your new life, and not someone new who doesn't know what you have been through."

I shook my head and smiled at the way she saw things.

"I have been hiding it for a month Kate, and he hasn't called or come by. I haven't received any phone calls of bitching from Maya. I feel like he dropped off the planet."

"Isn't that what you wanted?" Kate spoke softly as she walked across the endcap. "You told him you couldn't be his friend anymore so why are you driving yourself nuts with wondering why he hasn't popped back up."

I walked to the next aisle and ignored what she said. I knew she was right, but I didn't think Mark was the type to give up that easily.

"With Mark gone, Derrick keeps flying in and calls every night, and now Taylor wants to take me to a party. I feel like everything is happening really fast, but it's not," I whispered as I reached over and found a new purse that was a little bigger and cheaper that might work for her and held it up.

"Since you brought Taylor up, I want to tell you that I don't know how I feel about Taylor," Kate whispered without looking at the purse I was holding up. I lowered the purse and leaned across the display.

"How do you not know how you feel about someone?"

"Maybe I have turned paranoid from spending all this time with you, but hear me out. First we will start with the cryptic message RJ gave you, when he said he wasn't in it alone. That tells me the reason he has always seen everything is because there is a partner and to be honest I think it would have to be someone that could get close to you."

"Kate this is silly. They haven't found a shred of evidence that says that there was a second person helping him." I replied with annoyance.

"I am just saying RJ has green eyes, so does Taylor. You also need to consider that it took time to even figure out it was RJ. What if there is a second and he is better at hiding himself because he knows the system."

"Lots of people have green eyes, Kate." I stated with animosity at where this was going.

"What if you are flirting with Satan?"

"Taylor wouldn't betray me; he isn't like Eddie." I wished I could inhale the words back into my mouth. Bringing up her ex Eddie was not the way to make her feel better about Taylor.

"No Brooklyn, not everyone will be Eddie. He left me alone when my mom died, and that was more than a year ago. Taylor could be leading you to your death, it is not the same thing!" Kate exclaimed with disdain lining her words. "Plus, you cannot deny the fact that we all got shot except for Taylor!"

I closed my eyes and tried holding my breath to calm down, but she just kept talking "What about that threesome? You have never been that type of girl. You are upset about sleeping with a man who has someone else because you have that good girl mentality, but yet you brought someone else to your relationship before. And Taylor was just your boss. Now you're dating?"

I took another deep breath counted to ten in my head and looked at Kate. I then counted to a hundred because stopping at ten still left me with a raging need to scream at her. Not only was she adding to my paranoia, but she was pissing me off. I couldn't imagine anyone close to me being a psycho.

"Kate that was all me. I wanted to make Mark see what he would be missing without me. Taylor just happened to be there at the moment I needed to make my point."

"Did it work? Because last I checked you were still looking over your shoulder because that psycho got in your head. Then you have Taylor who is working himself to death and Mark is dating the police skank."

I blew out a breath I had been holding when my lungs began to burn. She wasn't wrong, but that didn't mean I needed the added stress of wondering who could be a traitor.

"Kate, we have to play the cards we are dealt. This is my hand, and I promise I won't fold, but I may not win. That is just the reality of my life. I want you to grow up and be respectful of the fact that I am going on this one date with Taylor and keep your conspiracy theories to yourself," I whispered and Kate looked shocked.

"You haven't allowed your heart to heal from Mark. Hell, you haven't even let your vagina heal."

"I was gone a year, Kate. What am I supposed to do? Am I supposed to pine away for a taken man? He is not coming back, Kate. He doesn't want me. He is happy with Maya."

I was growing more agitated the more we talked about it.

"Brooklyn, you are supposed to allow yourself time to heal or fight for what you want. If Taylor is what you want I will back down, but can you honestly look me in the eye and tell me you want him?" Kate spoke as her phone chimed.

She pulled up her phone as her tanned face paled instantly. She held it up to show me a picture of a woman tied up with familiar cuts from previous victims, but she was alive.

I walked over and stole her phone. I studied the background of the photo before reading the message. She was in a darkened tunnel and either she had wet herself or she was sitting in ponding water, but that was all I could make out in the picture. Then I read the message.

SEEMS BROOKLYN IS NOT THE ONLY ONE LEFT IN THE DARK. DO NOT DARKEN MY SUNSET OVER BROOKLYN OR THEIR WILL BE A FIERY HELL TO PAY.

Chapter Thirteen

Soon it was time to start getting ready to go. Taylor was usually the life of the party so I knew no matter what happened tonight I would have some fun, and my security was eager to go as they were outside dressed as R2-D2 and the Fonz.

RJ's text had caused me to have a mild panic attack, but I was starting to think the messages were not warnings, but a way to make me his puppet. I analyzed every line. The first sentence could mean that there was a new body they were hiding from me, or it may mean that I was actually going to be left in a darkened tunnel. The last line was familiar, he had said that before so had my dad.

It was frustrating that every time I got myself a little stronger a new note would come and knock me back down. I was even more determined now not to let his actions control my life. Tonight would prove he wasn't going to scare me anymore.

I showered and straightened my hair. I put on my white lace bra with my white lace panties and garter that came with the outfit. I even paired it with the white lace stockings.

Then I put on my nurse costume since he was taking me to a costume party downtown. I don't know why I was nervous, but my body was wriggled with anxiety.

My doorbell rang and I was strapping my white crisscross stilettos. I stood up and grabbed my pink stethoscope and threw it around my neck. I took a deep breath and opened the door.

"Holy shit, let's skip the party and let you take care of my new fever I got when you opened the door," Taylor said as he whistled.

"You like?" I asked spinning for him to see my white nurse's costume.

"Oh, I love," Taylor grabbed his heart and faked a heart attack. "Help me, I need to fall under your skirt and never get up."

"Taylor," I laughed at him as he crumbled to the floor in between my legs and rolled to look up my skirt.

"Just sit down, sweetheart and I will do the rest. We don't have to go anywhere. I swear I have died and am staring up into heaven."

"Well don't follow the white light yet, it is rude to die on a date," I stated with a laugh at his flirting.

"Princess Brooklyn, your chariot awaits," Taylor grunted as he climbed up off the floor. I finally got to take in his costume. He looked delectable as a Captain in the Army, as he was wearing ACU's.

"I'm a princess now? I thought I was a nurse," I spoke softly as I took in his tanned skin and green eyes glowed from the gray and green of the uniform. His black hair was a little too long to be a soldier, but I could see him being one if he wasn't already a prosecutor. He had those protective instincts that great soldiers seem to have.

"You are my princess. You defeated your own dragons to escape your ivory tower and rule the kingdom alone," Taylor spoke softly and I looked away because his flirting was turning serious and I wasn't ready for that. "Seriously Brooklyn, I am so proud of how you have handled yourself since your return. There were bets on how long you would last before you ran or before you went on a killing spree."

He pulled flowers, from his leg pocket and handed them to me. It was a small cropped bouquet of lavender roses. I ignored everything he had said and smiled as I brought them up to my nose to smell them.

"Thank you for the flowers, they are really pretty," I whispered.

"You ready to go, or do you want me to peel your thigh highs off with my teeth," Taylor asked and I placed a soft kiss on his lips.

"Take me out Taylor, but instead of the party I want you to show me something I would never see in the city."

"Well Miss Montgomery, I think I can rise to that challenge."

"Captain Taylor, I think you can rise to any challenge," I whispered with a wink as I walked out to change clothes.

"Hello," I answered my phone as I was getting dressed.

"Brook, I got that info you asked about," Derrick replied and I walked into my bathroom shutting the door to make sure I couldn't be heard.

"Well," I asked and Derrick let out a sigh.

"Sweetheart you are bait. There have been two more bodies that they have managed to keep away from the media and you. They are using the street department to block the scenes. The FBI wants to catch him as he is growing more unstable without your attention. Tonight's costume party is a ploy to get him to show himself. They have thirty cops going."

I sat on the toilet lid and a shiver ran through me. Kate was wrong about Taylor he wasn't trying to kill me, but he was prepared to use me as bait.

"We are not going," I replied as my world tilted. Who could I trust? Kate was too busy with Eddie. Mark might as well have a restraining order for the distance he kept between us. Derrick hadn't been in my life long enough and Taylor was using me to lure out the enemy. Taylor was going to catch him no matter the cost.

"Good, where are you headed?" Derrick asked in a rush as I heard his fingers snapping again.

"I don't know," I replied as my anxiety flourished.

"I have to go Brook, but text me when you get there so I know where you are."

When I hung up I felt very alone and was unsure of who I could turn to. Everyone wanted something or nothing from me.

"Where are we?" I asked as the salty ocean air flowed through my hair.

"The ocean," Taylor responded and shot me a smirk that said I will never tell.

"What are we doing out here?" I asked as he slowed the engine to the jet boat he had borrowed.

"You requested to see something that no one living in New York City will would see," I nodded my head as he shut off the motor to let us drift.

"Taylor I have seen the ocean a million times," I stated with my hands on my hips. I looked in the distance to see the police boat in the distance. Abbott and Costello were fishing and I couldn't help but smile.

Taylor turned out the main lights on the boat as we drifted further out into the ocean. He turned on the running lights and they lit up one by one near the benches at the front of the boat.

Taylor took my hand and led me to the benches, then he sat down. He pulled me down beside him. I snuggled up to him trying to find warmth as the chilling air bounced off the water. He may have been trying to use me as bait as the party, but out here I was safe.

"Brooklyn, lay down and close your eyes," Taylor ordered and I complied to see where this was going. I put my head in his lap and laid out on the benches.

"Taylor, your one job was to show me something I would never see in the city. Instead we are on a boat in the ocean. I see this every day."

"Well it took me a little bit, but I think I found something you will never see in the city."

I felt a blanket fall over me as I shivered under the cold ocean air. Even with my coat on the salty night air managed to chill me.

"Open your eyes Brooklyn and look straight up."

I complied and looked up to see the first star of the night had finally broke through the city lights and glowed down on the water. I was in awe that this is what he came up with and on such short notice.

"I wanted you to be granted any wish you felt like wishing."

"Taylor that is the sweetest thing," I whispered as I closed my eyes, Mark flashed through my mind at that very moment so I made a wish that this was the beginning of my broken heart healing. That I would be able to let Mark go, painlessly. I wished that Taylor could learn to talk to me about the things he plans, but had come to the conclusion he was worried about my mental state. I wished that RJ would get hit by a train, and I wished that I could find forgiveness for the pain I had caused my friends.

Before I opened my eyes I heard a bang and sharply sat up opened my eyes to see a ship bearing down on us. It seemed to be moving really fast.

"Taylor," I yelled as I pointed at the large rusted fisherman's ship that was bearing down on us rapidly. My heart raced as a spotlight suddenly shined down on our boat.

A loud clang sounded and I looked to see a newly formed hole in the boat right beside me. Another shot rang out and I screamed as smoke billowed out of our speakers on the overhead bars.

I heard the sirens of the police boat that Abbott and Costello were on as they headed toward us, but the fishing boat would get to us first.

"Get down," Taylor yelled as he crawled to the steering column, but another shot rang out and he fell to the floor.

"Taylor," I screamed as I watched the boat get closer. I looked over to see Taylor pulling out his phone as another bullet ricocheted and took out the light hanging on the upper bars.

"Brooklyn jump! Get off the fucking boat!" Taylor yelled and pointed to the side.

"Not without you," I screamed back as a fog horn echoed into the night sky. Taylor slowly got up on his knees and crawled toward me when another shot rang out. This time the windows shattered and I could feel warmth across my face. When the light shifted he stood up and charged at me. We both flew over the side of the boat.

The water was frigid and it felt like knives slicing into my body as I plunged into the cold dark waters. I struggled to get up to the surface, but my coat weighed a hundred extra pounds under water and I couldn't untie the petty coat to get loose.

I looked up as pieces of the boat Taylor had borrowed started falling into the water, and you could see fire on the surface.

I couldn't live like this. How many close calls would I have before my life was over? I had hurt everyone dying, and I hurt everyone returning. No one trusted me and I trusted no one. At that moment the thought crossed my mind that maybe being and staying dead was best.

I stopped fighting and just gave up. It was so easy to let go as the ice water had succeeded in stealing the air from my lungs as I started to sink. A tiny piece of me wanted to fight, but it pointless when dying was easier than living.

"Brooklyn stay with us," a voice called out as my chest cramped. My body jerked as someone punched me over and over in my chest. "Breathe sweetheart," The male voice called out as they pushed into me again. I coughed and swallowed water back into my lungs. I shivered as they rolled me on my side to spit out water.

"Get oxygen on her now," the voice called out and soon people were touching me from all directions. "Now that we got her back we need to get her to the hospital."

I didn't know the voices that spoke around me, and I had no energy to open my eyes. I tried, but I just couldn't force them open. My body wanted to sleep. I felt hands lift me onto some kind of cushion and the winds hit me as we moved.

"Get her in the ambulance and get her there now," a familiar voice called out, but I didn't know who it was. I felt like there was water trapped in my ears. I heard my own muffled groan as they shifted and jarred whatever I was on and it was only moments later I heard the ambulance sirens sound.

"Brooklyn, I need you to stay with me," a voice called out as I felt a cuff tighten on my arm. Darkness was ensuing and exhaustion was taking over. As I started to succumb to the sleep, my body so desperately wanted a voice called out.

"Brooklyn, can you look at me?" I felt a hand stroke my head as my body shook with chills. I was so cold, and so tired. I was trying to open my eyes, but they felt heavy and I didn't really want to. "Come on Brooklyn. Look at me. You don't get to end the game this way," the voice whispered into my ear and I opened my eyes to see the glowing green eyes and a crooked smile from RJ.

His hair was now black and a fake scar was peeling off his cheek. He wore an EMS Jacket that said his name was Kevin, but we both knew who he was. His lips moved, but I couldn't make out his words as tremors ran ramped through my body as I shook from fear.

I had to strain to catch what he was saying and it was taking more energy than I had. I grew lightheaded as his voice echoed in my ears.

"You don't get to die until the game is over. You don't get to die until I have you on your knees begging me for death. Stop being this weak imbecile because you don't get to die until we are done playing," RJ scolded.

"I never wanted to play-," I spoke silently as my energy depleted and darkness ensued me again.

A familiar beeping sound echoed in the background and a medicine dispenser grinded as I started to wake up. I could feel something plastic across my face and it laid inside my nose. I went to reach up to pull it out but my arms felt heavy.

I groaned as I tried again, but my arms wouldn't move.

"Brook,"

I heard Kate's voice and tried to talk, but it only came out as a grunt. I felt her hand in mine and squeezed as hard as I could. I heard some shuffling and then a beep sounded.

"This is the nurse how can I help you?" A voice sounded near the bed.

"Can you let the doctor know she is waking up?"

"We will page him and I will come in and check her vitals in a moment."

I didn't understand why I felt so sore and tired. I assumed I was in the hospital because the constant beeping was the same I heard when I had sat by Mark's bedside.

I crept my eyes open just a little and found myself in a darkened room. Kate was sitting on the edge of the bed holding my hand. I looked past her to see blue eyes popping out against the distance.

"Mark," I called out in a raspy voice.

"No, sweetheart it's Kate and Eddie," Kate said and I close my eyes and reopen them again. "Do you remember what happened?"

"Taylor?" I whispered as pain shot down my neck. I tried to clear my throat, but it burned.

"Taylor is fine. He got you out of the water and did CPR until they got you moved into the ambulance. Then you died again, but Eddie and his partner Kevin were able to get you back."

Kate brushed my hair off my face and I focused in on her face. The worry she carried across her face made her look older and exhausted.

"The boat," I whispered as the nurse came in the room and proceeded to check all my vitals. Kate stood up and stepped back but I squeezed her hand to make sure she stayed beside me. Once the nurse was done, Kate was at my side again and I saw Eddie wearing an EMT jacket in the light. Maybe I had hit my head because I didn't remember him being a medic.

"Brooklyn, the boat is in the bottom of the Atlantic Ocean."

I watched as Eddie put his hands on her shoulders in a supportive position. Kate let out a breath and wiped a tear from her eye.

"We have been talking and I think once we get you better you need to reconsider witness protection. The police and FBI said the ship was an accident that they didn't see you, but let's be honest you and I both know this was no accident. Taylor tells us someone was firing a gun at you both. Someone is still coming for you and they are not going to stop Brooklyn till you're dead."

Kate sat back on the side of the bed and I watched as Eddie placed his supportive hands around her body and rested his head on her shoulder.

"We already called Derrick and he is moving someone so he called someone here to come stay with you until he can get here."

"No more witness protection," I murmured groggily as the warmth from the medicine flooded my veins.

"Brook I don't think they are going to give you a choice. I heard the mayor talking to Taylor about the headlines that state: No lead into the attempted murder of the District Attorney and the Assistant District Attorney."

"Tell them no, Kate." I could barely stay awake, but needed her to stop them. "Tell them-," I never finished my statement as darkness took me under.

Chapter Fourteen

Two days later I got quizzed by Costello about what happened and while the details were a little fuzzy I remembered RJ in the ambulance. They looked at each other like I was crazy, but I wasn't, he was there.

I had just drifted off to sleep when the phone in my room rang.

"Hello," I answered groggily.

"How is my favorite witness?" Derrick replied and I smiled.

"I feel stupid," I replied. "They all think I am suicidal because it was just easier to let go than to fight in the water."

"Brooklyn were you trying to die?" Derrick asked with concern lacing his words.

"I don't think so," I whispered into the phone.

"What do you mean you don't think so?"

"When the water hit me it was like knives cutting my skin and my mind flashed to RJ and how that is what I would feel if he caught me. Then once he was in my head it just seemed easier to just let go and let whatever happens happen." I was lying about my reasoning, but I wasn't ready to admit that I had allowed myself to get that weak.

"Brooklyn, I think after what you have been through that is a normal reaction," even though I had been lying Derrick's response gave me a renewed strength that I wasn't crazy.

"You do," I whispered as shock rippled through me.

"Come on sweetheart think about it. You have been fighting to live for so long that when you associated the pain of his knife with the pain from the water you would rather let go than be tortured." Derrick rushed his words out as I heard movement in the background and someone was talking outside my door. "I am not a shrink, but I can understand why you felt that way, but never again are you to do that. I don't want to lose you."

Then there was a pause as I was rendered speechless.

"Want to tell me what happened in the ambulance?" Derrick asked and I cringed.

"They all think I am crazy, but he was there. He was demanding that I live to play with him. He pretty much called me a coward for giving up."

"Do you think maybe that was all in your head since he is the reason you gave up fighting in the water?"

"No, I saw him. I felt his demonic hands touch me. He was in the back of that ambulance demanding that I keep fighting," I replied and nearly sat up with anger when having to explain it to Derrick.

"Brooklyn I am not questioning it or you," Derrick let out a rush of air. "Listen to how it sounds: First you give up fighting because he got inside your head and it was easier to let go. Then he was in the ambulance demanding you keep fighting. It really sounds like the lack of oxygen in your brain from the water in your lungs made you hallucinate."

"He was there Derrick. He sat beside me demanding I live on."

"Brook, I have to go, but I believe you. If you say he was there, he was there. Remember you are not in this alone. If you need me I am there, and I called the NYPD and pulled a few strings to get someone much more capable than those other two to watch over you until I can get there. Then we will just talk about your options in witness protection."

I hung up and laid back as I tried to go to sleep once more. I was eager to make time pass so I could go home when my door opened to my room. I peeked through one eye to see that Mark had come into my room, and from the blanket and pillow he carried it looked like he was going to stay.

He walked over to the bench by the window that they had a cushion on as an extra bed and watched as his football player body tried to fit on it. After laughing at the way, he was trying to fold his body in half to fit I reached over and pressed the nurse call button.

"Nurse can I help you?" Mark looked at me and smiled.

"Can you bring a recliner bed for Detective Stone?" I asked as I returned his smile.

Within a minute or two they rolled one into the room and up beside my bed. I watched as Mark sprawled out in the chair as it laid back.

"Hi," I whispered without knowing exactly what to say. My mind went to places it shouldn't go because he was spoken for, but it went there anyway.

"Hi Brook," Mark responded. He wanted to say something it was written all over his face.

I watched his internal battle and decided to take the choice away from him and move the conversation away from whatever he was struggling to say.

"Are we having a sleepover?" I quietly asked as Mark laid there watching the news silently on the television.

"I just needed to know you are okay," Mark replied. "I didn't even know what happened until Derrick Stevens called me and asked me to keep a close eye on you until he could fly in."

"They think I am crazy," I murmured.

"I heard, but being paranoid after an event like that is normal." Mark reached over and placed his hand on mine.

"Being around you is hard," I whispered.

"I know," Mark responded as he turned to look at me. "You are going to have to get used to it because I am not going anywhere until you leave us again."

"Where am I going, Mark?" I asked because I had no intention of going anywhere.

"Derrick is coming to take you with him. He seems like a good man. He obviously cares for you and wants to protect you."

What can anyone say when the love of their life says they are better off with someone else? I said it all by saying nothing, but then the silence in the room nearly choking me. When quiet ensued my brain screamed out that I needed to get my shit together. I used the control to turn the volume up on the television.

"I heard you are with Taylor now," Mark spoke softly. "I am really happy for you."

That was enough of the bullshit small talk. I sat up as my body protested and turned off the television and turned on the lights. I glared at Mark before I spoke as I got my words together.

"No you are not happy for me. Let's get real for two minutes here," I started and Mark sat up. "You are not happy for me. I am not with Taylor. A date does not have some preordained meaning that you have to be with someone. If that were the case, I would be married to my vibrator as we have had a standing Monday night date for many years. Not that I have to explain anything to you."

I watched as Mark tried not to laugh, but I was serious as a heart attack.

"He kissed me. That is all. I mean seriously my toys get more action than that. And for you to think that you can come in here and sit there looking deliciously smug and say something like you are happy for me when I can see you want to shove a fist through a wall is worse than anything I have ever done, because at least I have been honest."

I paused to take a breath and Mark climbed up to sit on the bed where we were eye to eye. His close proximity threw me off my speech and I forgot what I was going to say.

"Don't stop now. I love seeing you be you." Mark smiled and chuckled as the monitor showed my heart rate increasing as my frustrations rose. "Calm down before the nurses come in here thinking you are having a heart attack," Mark whispered.

"I hate you," I whispered as Mark moved in closer to me.

"No you don't,"

"Yes, I really do." I whispered as his face was in front of mine. "I have to hate you."

"Prove it! Tell me to stop. Tell me no." Mark whispered and I couldn't say a word. He was going to kiss me I just knew he was.

"I can't," I whispered as Mark moved in and no sooner than he put his lips on mine the doctor walked in. *What does a girl have to do to get laid?*

"You are going home. The nurses are working up your discharge paperwork, and will come remove your IV and such soon. For the next couple days, I want you to rest. Stay in bed. Read a book. Watch television."

"Hey Doctor, if I promise to stay in my room can we stay here tonight and go home in the morning? It is already dark and I don't want to go home alone."

The doctor nodded his head and ordered me to get some sleep. Mark moved back to the recliner and laid down. I turned out the light and we watched some old black and white movie in silence.

As the movie came to an end, I looked over to see Mark was sleeping.

"Hey Mark," I whispered and he didn't budge. With him asleep I had the courage to say the words I needed to get off my chest. "Tonight will be the last time you see me. We obviously can't stop pushing the line between right and wrong when we see each other. I need to be happy so whether that is with Derrick or Taylor or someone new or if RJ kills me tomorrow, it doesn't matter because we need to be free of each other. I don't know why I keep holding on to the memory of you, but I have to let you go and you have to stay away."

I didn't hear a thing and was a little relieved saying it out loud, but it also made it very real. I turned my back to him and silently cried as I realized that I was losing my best friend again.

"Brooklyn," Mark started and I knew he had heard me. When I didn't answer him, I heard the recliner adjust and thought he was getting up to leave, but instead he curled up next to me and wrapped his arm around me as I cried.

"Why can't we just go back to the way things used to be?" Mark asked and I did my best to slow my tears. I turned in his arms and looked at him. His blue eyes knew exactly how to make me feel loved or cut me like a knife as they were doing now.

"Why can't there be a rewind button or an elevator that takes us back to when we were five years old when life was simple and we had no worries. I would love to take you back there. Take you to a time where no one wanted to hurt you and we could just be us," Mark whispered then he placed a kiss on my forehead. I could only shake my head at him and his thought pattern because we both knew that could never happen.

"Once a month," Mark started talking again and I pulled back to look at him with confusion on my face as I swiped at my remaining tears. "Once a month, you and I are going to rent a bouncy house or a laser tag place, or any fun zone and we are going to meet there. You can be my mini-golf mistress," Mark stated and I burst out laughing.

"There is the smile I love to see. No more tears over me. I am not worth it," Mark spoke softly.

"What if I am in witness protection?" I asked since Derrick had called him and told him what happened.

"Then I guess I better suck up to the Marshals and start working on clearances."

"Where does Maya think you are tonight?" I asked with genuine curiosity.

"She knows I came to stay here with you after what happened."

"She didn't throw a fit?" I asked because her personality said otherwise.

"She threw a bunch of things to include my keys and that is how I got here. She will calm down before I see her tomorrow. She doesn't do well with people who still live in my heart."

"Mark we can't sneak off to a play world. It is wrong, and both Maya and I would have to be okay with sharing your time and I can tell you I don't want to share your time or see you with her. Not now, not ever."

"Shh, my bouncy castle princess, it is time for you to rest. Just let me hold you tonight and if you still feel that way in the morning I will be gone, and I won't push our blast from the past meetings."

Dream

"Hello," I called out as I walked down the white hallway. My heels clicked on the floor as they had done so many times before, but there was no one chasing me. There were no footsteps or bleeding walls. There was no floating floors or carousels.

I walked down the hallway eager to find the red door. With no one out to get me maybe I could find Heaven behind the door. The closer I got I heard a piano playing in the distance it was a creepy version of a lullaby with the sound of children's laughter all around.

As I came to the red door I turned the knob and opened it to a bright light that shined down on me. I closed my eyes and tuned out the laughter as I basked in warmth.

"You shouldn't be here," a familiar voice called out. "I raised you better than that."

I opened my eyes to see my mom and dad embracing before me in the light.

"Mom?" I spoke softly. "Dad?"

"This is not the ending for you. You need to choose another door," my mom spoke up as an added light shined down on her to show her angelic wings and her inner beauty.

"You are not destined for this place with us. You have to fight the devil to enter the Heavens. You have not fought the demon and won. If you die now you live inside him forever," my dad replied as he reached a hand out to me.

"Daddy, I am so sorry," I cried and reached for him but he was drifting away from the door. "Please forgive me for not saving you."

"Pick another door," my dad replied and gave me a final wave as they were sucked into the darkness and there was nothing behind the door. There was nowhere to go as the door ripped from my hand and sealed itself shut.

I wiped the tears from my eyes and listened to the sounds of laughing children chiming along with the beats to the eerily familiar nursery rhyme.

I walked back a few doors until the sound was louder. I placed my hand on the doorknob and opened it. I walked into a torch-lit room walking through cobwebs as I entered what looked like Dracula's chamber with black walls with dripping blood and a coffin in the room.

I walked up to the coffin to see myself laying inside. I reached out and placed a hand on myself to feel how hard and cold I was. *How was I dead?* A familiar laugh caught my attention and I turned around to see an open area around the corner.

I walked forward and turned the corner to see the man from the podium, the dragon, sitting at a piano playing music. I continued to walk through the entryway until I could see the rest of the room.

I stood in shock as light filled the room from a window and I could see children lining the walls in spider cocoons. As a boy skipped and danced to the music, a large black widow came down and rolled him into her web as the child laughed with glee as if it was a game.

"What are you doing?" I demanded to know.

"Ahh Brooklyn, so nice to see you again," the man stood up from the piano, but the notes kept playing. "I don't think you are ready for me," he issued out the information as if it was a challenge.

"What are you doing to those kids?" I glared at him. He took a few steps toward me and I watched his eyes turn from a glowing green to a black.

"Watch," he ordered and my body instantly faced the wall and I couldn't look away. I watched as a blond girl came in and played hopscotch as the song played, and when it paused she looked at me covered her mouth and laughed.

My eyes were frozen to her as my heart sunk. It was a little Maya. She was maybe five years old with pigtails. She was so happy and free until blood started dripping out of the piano and the tune changed.

The giant widow came now and snatched her up, and climbed her about half way up the wall where she placed her in the web and Maya giggled as the spider spun her over and over again.

"Are you going to kill them?" I asked as I took in all the souls that were hanging on the wall.

"Yes, I will eat them alive," the spider spoke as his face changed into the man's who had been standing right beside me. "I take them and string them up. As they fight to live I toy with them taking out the parts I don't want.

Then I start at their feet and eat them until I have their soul."

"Sounds familiar," I whispered and the spider smiled. "That is what you did to me, yet here I am."

"You are here because I want to play a game with you," the spider's words echoed and a shiver traveled down my spine.

"I don't play games," I retorted as my heart rate leapt with the closeness of his body to me.

"You have been playing them all along," the spider took in his wall as if he had accomplished something good, and I wanted to vomit thinking of how badly those people had suffered.

I walked into the room and the little girl was no longer laughing. She was starting to cry and panic as she realized she couldn't get loose.

"She is just a child. You can't have her soul."

"That is a myth Brooklyn. I can have whatever I want and there is nothing you can do to stop me," the spider spoke as I took in the room looking for a weapon or something to cut her down.

I ran for a torch on the wall to turn and wave it at nothing. The spider was gone. I went over to the wall and began burning the web. The hundreds of kids disappeared and only Maya was left.

"Help me," she called out to me as the silk tightened down the more she wiggled. "Please save me," she pleaded.

Those words were like nails on a chalkboard as I knew something bad was about to happen. I turned to look behind me only to see I was completely encased inside a web on every side. I tried to burn it but the fire merely turned it crimson and the blood of the victims poured off the silk lines.

I turned back around to see Maya was gone. *Where the hell did she go?* I instinctively spun around and prayed for a giant can of Raid or a boot. I heard a laugh come from above me and turned my attention up to the ceiling to see the spider coming down for me.

I waved the torch, but it mysteriously turned to water and splashed over the floor. *Where the hell was a rolled up magazine when you need one?* In one swift move, I was in the spider's legs being carried high up on the wall.

I kicked and scream and fought to get loose, but his legs merely tightened down around me.

"You wait till I find bug spray!" I screamed and the web shook with the room and I thought it was an earthquake, but instead the floor opened up and a pool of sharks spun below as I was being carried up.

I watched as the shark's pool turned into lava and they swam around in it as they turned black and their eyes glowed red. *What the fuck?* I panicked and reached for the web and held on as the spider tried to pull me away.

"I guess you are not going to go quietly into the night," the spider spoke and I saw the crimson lion enter the room from a new door with a smile for me. Then the dragon who was as tall as the room smiled from across the room.

"How many?" I bellowed as the spider tried to pull me away from the hold I had. "How many of them are you?"

"More than you can count," the dragon growled with a raspy voice. "We are everywhere. We live in the corners in your house. We live in the nursery rhymes you grow up with. We are on your television, in your imagination, and in your soul."

My body began spinning as the spider wrapped me in his silken web. I tried to pull away, but the more I moved the faster I was left immobile and unable to defend myself.

"I am used to you killing me," I spat out as rage covered the fear I felt.

"I know," the dragon laughed. "That is why you get to watch people die."

I watched as a five-year-old version of me, Mark, Kate, Maya, and Taylor entered the room. I screamed for them to run, but they never even looked my way.

"Tell me Brooklyn, when it is your turn how do you want to go out or shall I choose something extra special just for you?" The spider whispered in my ear as he spit something that burned my flesh over the silk.

"Fuck you," I screamed as the kids all stopped and stared up at me. "Run," I screamed as they laughed. The dragon had returned back into his human form and walked over and took Mark's hand.

When I felt the first bite from the spider I closed my eyes and looked away as Mark disappeared over the lava sharks. I screamed in agony as I felt my organs being sucked out one by one and the demon picked up Kate.

"Please, don't hurt them," I screamed and a bright light shined down into the room as the demon sat Kate down for the lion to pounce on. "Please," I begged as the excruciating pain pulled at my chest.

I turned to look with my head to see the spider was sucking my heart out of my chest as he discarded my ribs one by one. "Leave them alone."

"I warned you that you were not ready for me. You didn't even put up half the challenge you have before."

Then I rose out of the coffin and my body grew into a large maroon dragon. I watched as the dragon laughed at me. Then I watched as the dragon version of me came forward and moved in to bite down on my face.

"Ahh," I screamed.

"Brooklyn, you're okay," Mark held me as I took in my surroundings. I was still in the hospital. "Close your eyes, and get some rest I am right here." Then Mark sang to me till I calmed down enough to settle back into him. I had to get RJ out of my head before I went insane.

Chapter Fifteen

The next week I started working from home. I was able to access the system from my laptop and it was easier for me to write briefs all day every day if I was at home where I felt more comfortable and wasn't looking over my shoulder. Running around in my pajamas were a plus too.

Taylor worried about me and called from time to time, but I kept getting the impression he wanted more from me than I was prepared to give. He was part of my fall out with Mark and seeing him brought that day to the surface all over again every time I saw him.

A knock sounded on my door and I walked over to answer it. I smiled when I saw Derrick standing in the door with red roses and a bottle of wine.

"Dinner?" He asked and I opened the door further to let him in. He was dressed in jeans and a Red Sox t-shirt with a leather jacket. It didn't really look like dinner apparel.

"I am not really dressed for dinner," I replied taking in my white tank top and gray sweatpants. I had on no make-up and my black hair was up in a messy bun on my head.

"I anticipated that when I heard you were becoming a hermit," Derrick replied and he sat the wine and roses down on the island. He took off his leather jacket and I glanced at the excitement in his brown bedroom eyes before he went to the door and opened it. Men in white dovetail jackets came in and set up my tiny two seater table with a table cloth and candles.

They flourished my floor with rose petals and glitter confetti in the shape of hearts and stars. The men laid out a feast on the island in silver trays. They placed three level dessert trays on my coffee table as they were flourished with chocolate covered strawberries and tiny finger cakes.

My apartment smelled of gourmet cooking. Even Abbott and Costello were drooling from my door. After everything was set in a romantic scene, I was sure he stole from some movie the men in coats left and I was alone with Derrick.

"What is this?" I asked taking in the view.

"Just a little dinner," Derrick smiled and I laughed.

"You know you are cleaning this up right?" I asked and Derrick laughed and nodded his head. He lit candles all around my open floor plan and lowered the lights as we made our plates and sat down together to eat.

The dinner conversation was as if it were an actual date it was all "tell me about your day," and "what do you do for fun." When we finished, I made plates for Abbott and Costello and delivered it to them outside my door.

"Dance with me Brooklyn," Derrick called out as I started to clean up.

"There is no music," I replied with a smile and he walked over to me and took my hand and led me away from the kitchen to the open area near the entryway, where Mark had danced with me and he spun me out and brought me back in as he took me in his arms.

There in the silence of the night I danced with Derrick. He spun me out and brought me back in to dip me, and there leaning back I loosened my grip on his arm and allowed trust to flow through me.

Derrick pulled me back up and we were nose to nose swaying to an imaginary beat.

"I want to kiss you," Derrick whispered and I balled his t-shirt into my fists and licked my lips. He tilted his head and placed his lips over mine. A sudden rush of confusion enveloped me. My brain kept saying this is the way to move on and my heart kept screaming out for Mark.

Derrick's cinnamon flavor wasn't Mark's coffee and whipped cream, but I wouldn't be with Mark again so I had to shake him from my mind.

Derrick was not like Mark, he didn't just grab and take what was his, and that was exactly what I wanted. I didn't want to be inside my own head. I didn't want to make any more decisions. I just wanted someone to take all the outside world away from me for an hour and make me feel cherished.

I placed my hands on Derrick's chest and pushed him back.

"I can't get him out of my head," I whispered and stared at the floor. Derrick placed his fingers under my chin to make me look at him as tears filled my eyes.

"I'm not him, Brooklyn I will never be him. I will never hurt you or make you shed a tear over me. I told you that you are not in this alone, and I intend to stay as long as I am allowed," Derrick spoke softly and then pulled me into his arms.

"It is just so hard to let go," I sobbed into his chest. "He had an entire year to move on and I feel like we just ended."

"Maybe some time away will do you some good," Derrick whispered as he laid his chin on top of my head.

"That is what got me into this," I wiped my tears with my hand in a very unladylike way. Derrick merely smiled and pushed the strands of my hair that had fallen out of my face.

"I won't tell you I love you. I won't make you promises of rainbows and sunshine. I won't give you hearts and flowers. All I can give you is me and hope that it is enough to be a bridge to walk away from him and stay with me," Derrick spoke softly, and the words rushed over me telling me that I needed to stop listening to my heart and just go with it.

I wrapped my arms around Derrick's neck and pulled his lips to mine. I deepened the kiss pushing my tongue into his waiting mouth to massage his. He grabbed my butt and started walking me backward to the bedroom, but I couldn't go in there.

I pushed his chest and walked him into the laundry room. I pulled my tank over my head and threw it in the washer and then I did the same with my sweats and panties. I took a deep breath as I had not been naked with anyone without Mark in a long time.

"You're stunning," Derrick whispered as I reached for his shirt. I threw it in front of the washer and went for his jeans. Within minutes, we were both standing naked in the laundry room and I turned on the washer to start my load.

Derrick wasted no time pushing me up against the washer and planting a kiss on my neck. I ran my hands down his chest that showed the slightest hints of a six pack. He had started hitting the gym hard when we hit Tennessee and it was starting to show.

He moved his hands to my nipples and gave them the slightest tug. He was no longer treating me as a delicate flower and for that I was grateful.

By the time, the washer was shaking the water back and forth to clean my clothes Derrick turned me to face the washer and bent me part of the way over. He pulled my hair and bit my neck as his hand found my opening and pushed two fingers inside.

I moaned out and Derrick dropped to his knees to lick my opening from behind me. I cried out when his tongue found my clit as his fingers continued to fuck me.

"You are so sweet," Derrick mumbled. For a split second, I got lost in the moment and nearly called out Mark's name. The words he used were so close to what Mark always said. I bit my lip, but Mark's face flashed through my mind.

I stood up and pulled Derrick up to me. I needed to be able to see his face. He pulled a condom from his wallet and I ripped it open with my teeth. I used my hands to push it down his hardened penis.

"Wrap your legs around me," Derrick growled and I complied pushing my back against the dryer and finding Derrick at my entrance. "You ready?" He asked and I merely nodded.

Derrick pushed into me so slowly and I kept my lip in between my teeth to keep me from saying anything as sweat broke out across my body. I was raging with hormones, but I just wasn't climbing the climax mountain like I did with Mark.

Derrick pushed the button on my dryer and the motor roared to life. I moaned as the vibration shook him inside me. Derrick pushed in and out of me and lifted my knees enough to hit that rough patch over and over again.

I closed my eyes and allowed my body to take over as my brain took me to new heights.

The smell of sex filled the air as I felt him pull my hair back exposing my neck. He then placed his hand on my throat and gave it the slightest squeeze.

A rush of adrenaline coursed through my body as fear cascaded along my nerve endings. I opened my eyes to look at him. He laid a kiss on my lips and tightened his grip on my throat.

"Derrick," I rasped out. "Derrick," I called out as panic enveloped me. He stopped his movements and took his hand down as I shivered with anxiety.

"Brooklyn, I won't hurt you," he whispered and I felt foolish. I have had sex before when a man did that. It was supposed to increase pleasure, but instead it left me wishing I was anywhere else. "Brooklyn, talk to me," Derrick whispered.

"I can't," I whispered and pushed away from him. Once he pulled out of me and sat me down I ran to my bathroom and locked myself inside. I couldn't face him. I overreacted with his touch, and I had been thinking of Mark. I was not ready for this.

I felt dirty so I stood in the shower for what felt like years. The water was ice cold by the time I shut it off. I put on my robe and walked out into my bedroom. I didn't hear any movement and I was hoping he was gone.

I walked into my living room to see that all the food had been cleaned up and there was a card folded on the island next to the flowers. I walked over and picked it up.

Brooklyn,

I am sorry if I pushed you too hard or too fast. I was so eager to get inside you that I didn't even think of how you were feeling.

I didn't consider your pleasure or your emotions.

You are like an addicts dream. You are strong and beautiful. You are funny and stubborn.

You are all the makings of the perfect woman. I know your heart is hurting right now, but always remember that just because he didn't want you doesn't mean you are not just right for someone else.

I am going to give you some space, but know that I am merely a phone call away and that you are never alone.

Derrick

Chapter Sixteen

"Seriously, Brooklyn!" Kate exclaimed as I walked around my open floor plan apartment in my pink tank top and my black shorts. My cold hardwood floors had me on my tiptoes as I exited my bedroom and headed for the kitchen.

"It has only been a week. I am just not ready to go back out there. I needed a time out." I explained as I walked into the kitchen to make a fresh pot of coffee and refill Abbott and Costello's coffee mugs.

"Tell me what happened to you between last week and this week," Kate demanded and I opened my mouth and explained what happened with Derrick.

"Woah honey I am going to stop you right there. Men can fuck around to move on, but us women, well it doesn't work like that. You can screw the entire world tonight, but in the morning you are still going to be head over heels for Mark."

I nodded my head because I knew what she was saying was true, but I had allowed myself to trust Derrick when we were dancing, but I couldn't when he was inside me. That was a riddle to me.

"I am going to become agoraphobic and never leave the apartment again," I joked as I picked up the mail and saw my invitation to the policeman's ball. I opened the pristine invitation that said the mayor demanded my presence. Nothing like getting forced to go to a party when you want to be a hermit.

"Brooklyn, are you listening? I am going to call the psych ward. I have been patient with you, but you haven't left your apartment in seven days. No matter what happened, this is not healthy. You need to come party with me."

I rolled my eyes as I stood next to the island in the kitchen. Kate stood with her hands on her hips in her jeans and a black tank top showing her electronically sun-kissed skin. Her blond hair flowed down her mid back and her blue eyes glared at me.

I walked to the window and pulled back my gray curtains and looked out at New York lights that brightened as the sun sat lower in the sky.

"He is out there watching me. He is waiting for me to step outside. He will be out there tonight looking for what could be his next victim. I always felt safe when I was with Mark, but out there alone-," I stopped talking turned and looked at Kate "Maybe tomorrow I will go, but tonight I won't be his so I am staying in."

"What happened to my best friend? The one who defied the odds and kicked everyone's ass? The one who came home to live her life? Looks like you are hiding at home, instead of living, and RJ hasn't done anything like he had before. You put him inside your head and you have left him there. He is sitting back laughing at the fact that you are doing more damage to yourself than he could ever do to hurt you. Maybe he thinks the new you is boring and he wants to play with someone else."

I started to speak when my phone chimed a familiar tune. Before I could get back into the kitchen to pick it up Kate snatched the phone from the counter and began Face Timing with Taylor.

"Taylor, I swear to God I am going to kidnap her. If the apartment complex burns down I think she would go down with it rather than step outside."

I could hear Kate complaining as she walked into my bedroom with the phone. I shook my head as I turned and grabbed the coffee pot. I walked to the door and opened it to see a smile from Abbott and Costello.

"Ms. Montgomery, you know if you want to go out we will be there this time. Nothing will happen to you on our watch." Abbott announced as I poured Costello's coffee. I knew they felt guilty about the accident, but who could have guessed he would have been ready with a boat when it was a spur of the moment decision. I asked Taylor to take me somewhere else, there was no way anyone would know I would do that.

"Sorry, she is being so loud. I appreciate the offer, but I am fine in my apartment. I have plenty of work to do," I spoke in a whisper.

"I have to agree with your friend in there. You seem to have lost your edge. We kind of miss the challenge in trying to keep up with you," Costello spoke softly, as if I was still fragile.

I just smiled up at him. I finished filling the coffee mugs and walked back inside the apartment. I stopped in my tracks as Kate held up a black strapless dress.

"Taylor is going to help me cover up your extraction so I won't go to jail. Your security detail is being informed now as you have two choices. You can come out willingly or I have permission to break the law you love so much and kidnap you."

Oh hell, this was not going to end well. Kate with a dress and me with a hot pot of coffee.

"Dating in New York City should be considered a crime."

I whined as I sat in my black strapless dress with my back in a brown leather booth and suffered through speed dating with Kate on my left and a woman who wouldn't stop crying on my right.

The darkened restaurant seemed to attract the creepy people who liked speed dating. Just like the crooked-nosed pervert in front of me who wanted to know if he could suck my nose. *Ugh*.

I looked over at Kate tossing her blonde hair showing the scar alongside her neck that I would always feel responsible for.

"Do you really hate this?" Kate quietly asked while her date in a suit coat and jeans began chewing on his fingers like it was all you can eat at KFC. *Gross.*

"No, I guess it's not awful, but what about Eddie?"

"Brooklyn, do you want to leave?" Kate asked quietly ignoring the mention of her boyfriend as we heard the timer buzz again.

"No, we can stay a little longer if you want too." I replied as my next date sat down. He had a purple and black Mohawk and large holes in his ears and lip. His eyes were completely white with the help of his contacts. The tattoos all across his body made me think he was an artist of some type, but the parole anklet said I needed to steer clear.

"So, what is your name?" The tattooed artist asked.

"I'm Brooklyn and what is your name?"

"They call me Clone," he stated proudly.

"Who calls you Clone?" I ask knowing I probably didn't want the answer.

"Everyone does. I am famous," he replied and I wanted to ask what he was famous for, but decided against it. In his mind, he was famous, but in reality I doubted it.

"Why do they call you Clone?" I asked curiously.

"Because I can clone myself into whoever's flesh I eat."

What the fuck did he just say? Suddenly I regretted telling Kate we could stay. Now would be time to run away and go back to the safety of my apartment. I shivered as I watched him lick his lips.

"Is this seat taken?" A familiar voice asked my two-minute date. I looked up and was graced with a beautifully tanned Taylor, who was all smiles for me. I looked at my date and since he didn't get up, I felt I should say something.

"I see no reason why we should finish this *agonizing* two-minute date. I mean no offense when I say this, but I am sure you are a five-pump-chump kind of guy and well, I take my time. Neither of us would get any *satisfaction* with the other. I think you should step aside and let the grown-ups talk for a minute."

My two-minute date growled at Taylor as he stood up to walk away and I tried to stifle my laughter. It felt good to be out in the open now that I was having a little fun. It felt amazing for that one glimmering moment to be the person I used to be. Taylor sat at the table and smiled a genuinely happy smile for me before nodding his head in Kate's direction.

"Miss, you are the most beautiful woman in the room." Taylor announced loudly just as Kate cleared her throat in his direction. My heart raced as all eyes were on me. "What I meant to say was I am in the best place because I am near the two most beautiful women in the room."

I forced a laugh as he reached for my hand and laid a kiss on my knuckles.

"What are you doing here?"

"I am rescuing the fair maiden from a life of bad dates and awful sex," Taylor retorted with a whisper and a smirk.

Boredom and unease had sunk in before he had arrived, but I was sure that would change. As the buzzer sounded again, I wondered what he had in store for us.

"May I have your attention? Please," Taylor yelled as he dropped my hand and stood up. "I am merely looking for females to join me for a threesome. Any takers?"

Kate and I smiled at each other and then stood up. Taylor held out his elbows and we linked our arms in his. The woman on the other side of me slapped her date and wanted to know why in the two seconds they had sat together he hadn't tried to get in her pants. I burst out laughing as we started toward the exit

Men stood to applauded Taylor. Wolf whistles echoed throughout the room and Taylor merely nodded his head while Kate and I pretended to swoon. As soon as we got out the door Taylor released Kate and pulled me into a hug.

"It's been a long while since I saw you out, baby girl. How are you doing?"

"I'm good Taylor," I smiled at him.

"Guys this has been fun, but I am going to sneak off. I texted Eddie and he is home so it is time to get my nightly sexy man fix."

Taylor and I both gave Kate a hug and said our see ya later's, as I kept quiet about what I thought about Eddie. It was a pure struggle not to call him names or want to kick him in the balls whenever he was around, but I was respectful of what my best friend wanted.

"Seriously Brooklyn, how are you doing out here? You look really nervous and that is not like you," Taylor whispered as I saw Abbott and Costello waiting outside the restaurant for us.

"I am fine," I lied and faked a smile.

"Brooklyn, be honest with me. I feel like you aren't talking to me, that you have been talking at me. You aren't letting me in or letting me help," Taylor whispered as he held my hand. I sighed I guess I needed to unload on someone. Maybe I would no longer be his bait if he knew how I felt.

"I feel like I can't trust anyone and that you all see me as a burden instead of a friend. Everyone moved on with their lives and it left me trying to play catch up. I somehow thought coming home I would lose the anxiety, but it has only grown since we were shot at."

"Brooklyn give it time. We all heal differently. You can't expect everything to go back to normal just because you are home and your hair is black again. It doesn't work that way. Life went on without you, and now you just got to let it catch back up to you," Taylor muttered as he pushed my black hair back behind my shoulder to notice the new tattoo. I took a deep breath as he stared at it as though it would communicate to him what it meant.

"I am just scared all the time. It is déjà vu. Abbott and Costello following me. I am always looking around to see when he might approach me. He hasn't done anything to warrant the fear in me in a while, but yet waiting for him to replenish the fear is exhausting."

"I think you need a drink. Would you like to get a drink with me, Miss Montgomery?" Taylor asked as he extended his elbow for me to take. I don't know why, but at that moment I looked in Abbott and Costello's direction and they nodded their approval to go out. I took a deep breath and decided to go with it.

"Why yes, Mr. Cross, I would like that."

The night air in New York had chilled and I shivered as I stopped to take off my heels. Taylor never took his glowing green eyes off me. For a second RJ's words flashed in my head, *"I was never in this alone."*

"Are you cold?" Taylor asked and I nodded my head as he wrapped his jacket around me and we walked up the steps of the public library. One stop on the way to the bar at my favorite place wouldn't hurt.

"Taylor how did you know where I would be tonight?"

"Kate told me where she was taking you and why. Plus, anyone on the force can find you with Abbott and Costello on your tail."

"Why did you show up?" I asked as I sat on the steps next to the stone lion outside the New York City public library. I looked past Taylor and saw a man coming towards us quickly. My body began to shiver and my reaction said to run. I no longer heard anything that Taylor said as this man in dark clothes closed in on us.

"Ahhh," I screamed frozen in place as the man dropped a rose into my lap. I immediately shoved it off me as if it was burning me, and climbed up the stairs of the library. I was not all right, I had let RJ into my soul like the demons in the dreams and he was sucking the life out of me. Every time I thought I was okay I wasn't, and the worst part was I couldn't blame RJ because I had allowed him to stay in my head.

"Brooklyn – sweetheart." Taylor began saying things but his voice sounded muffled, I couldn't understand. The roses, we never investigated as to why RJ gave them roses. *Did the second man give them the roses?* I was gasping for air as the man took off.

I shivered and slid one arm into the sleeve of Taylor's jacket. I looked down and looked at the scar I wore on my arm from RJ shooting me before sliding my other arm in. It was my reminder that no matter how much you think you're safe you never are. Everyone was RJ in my mind and I was wearing a big flashing neon bull's-eye on my back.

"Taylor, I really need to go home."

Abbott went for the car, as Costello was on the phone.

"Brooklyn, you are all right. He was just trying to make some money by selling flowers. You're shaking, maybe you should stay with me tonight," Taylor whispered as the SUV pulled up.

"I can't. I have to go home."

"Are you going to isolate yourself in your ivory tower?" I didn't answer because I didn't know how I would feel when I came up from the fear and down from the adrenaline.

"Brooklyn, listen very carefully to me. If you stay inside, he wins. If you give up on life, he wins. If you admit defeat, guess what happens?" Taylor asked.

"He wins," I whispered

"Why don't you take me on a real date sometime?" I asked softly. "One where no one tries to kill us."

Taylor smiled and reached for my hand and kissed my knuckles then nodded his head. Then he walked me over to the SUV and helped me inside.

"I will call you tomorrow," Taylor stated before shutting the door and we headed home.

Chapter Seventeen

Abbott and Costello got me home just minutes before there was a knock on my door. I opened it to see Mark standing there looking like his normal handsome self in a gray button down and a pair of jeans. He must have been working the area as his badge was hanging around his neck.

"What are you doing here?" I asked with confusion. I thought we agreed to stay away from each other.

"You okay?" He asked and I opened my door further to let him walk inside.

"Why wouldn't I be okay?" I asked and he crossed his arms and gave me that detective look that said he knew everything.

I walked past him and put on a pot of coffee. He stood stoic as I went into my bedroom and changed out of the dress, and put on a black tank top and my pink shorts and put my hair up in a messy bun.

"I heard you met Clone," Mark muttered with a smirk.

"That guy is creepy," I retorted.

"He has his moments, but he has been a good CI for us."

"He is your confidential informant? That piece of garbage works for you?" I asked with shock thinking of how that guy would ever work out on the stand in a courtroom.

"Want to talk about what happened tonight?"

"Here we are again," I said under my breath as I poured two coffee cups. Mark chuckled and I watched him get up and walk over to the refrigerator that was basically empty except for creamer and yogurt. He looked back at me.

"You know I learned a lot about you in the twenty years or so we have known each other."

"Oh, yea and what is it you think you know," I asked as he closed the refrigerator.

"A beautifully broken Brooklyn is a skinny Brooklyn."

"What?" I asked because that made no sense to me.

"Brooklyn, you are the most beautiful woman I have ever seen in my life, but when you break you stay shattered. When you are left in pieces, you stop taking care of yourself.

Hence, the reason you are skin and bones and there is barely any food in your house."

Mark then sipped at his coffee on the island as I sat and waited for him to finish so I could defend myself.

"Brooklyn I know you don't want to be friends and I am trying to respect that, but you seem like you are walking a tightrope and I want to help you stay balanced."

Mark walked over and sat on the navy blue couch that I loved so much. He patted it as in saying come over and sit down.

"I haven't gone shopping," I whispered.

"Because you have decided to let fear take over your life and stay indoors." Mark opened his shirt and showed me his scar. "Brooklyn I got shot. I died and woke up to learn the one woman I could truly be with was dead. Then I got better and I went back to work, and I found a new woman to share my life with. Life goes on if you let it. Now tell me what happened tonight."

"I just got a little freaked out by this guy with roses and then Taylor was being a little pushy when I just wanted to come home. It was my own fault."

I stood up and began to pace, which had become common when I didn't know what to do with my nervous energy.

"Brooklyn -," Mark said as he put his coffee down and stood up. "Brooklyn I won't let him get to you," then Mark pulled me into his arms and I held onto him as if he were a life saver in the middle of the ocean. "They put two of the best detectives at your door tonight. Detective Matson, and Monroe so Abbott and Costello can have some down time. They won't let anyone inside this apartment."

I held onto the wall of muscle that was the Mark I knew and drooled over. He placed a kiss on my head then he pulled me back and took my hand and led me to the bedroom. "You don't need coffee Brooklyn, you need a good night's sleep, and breakfast that doesn't come in a yogurt container in the morning. You will feel better and be more in control when you sleep."

I crawled into the bed and Mark pulled my blue comforter up and then sat on the side of the bed. His jaw was clenching and he seemed to be deep in thought when I reached out and took his hand.

"Can you stay till I fall asleep?" I asked and Mark nodded he walked around the other side of the bed and climbed in on top of the comforter. I rolled and turned my body to face him as he draped one arm across my body.

I reached into the covers where the remote control had been left and handed it to him. I closed my eyes and drifted off to sleep as Mark watched television into the night.

The hours had passed and like normal I was dreaming that I was standing before the devil. I felt the agony and pain from everyone who had been subjected to RJ's knife because I wasn't strong enough to stop him. *I was never strong enough.*

"Brooklyn-," Mark called out into my dream. "Brooklyn, wake up," he said and gave me a shake. I opened my eyes and started to sob.

"He always finds me, and everyone always dies," I muttered into Mark's chest.

Mark, who was now under my comforter as the apartment had chilled to near frigid temps, held me tightly to him and let me cry. When I had no more tears to give the demons, I pulled back and looked at Mark. The concern in his eyes was evident, and I knew he was going to say something like 'you need therapy' and I didn't want to hear it.

I pushed myself forward and placed my wet tear stained lips to his hot velvety ones. He pulled back a moment and studied my face, and then his lips crashed into mine. It was hard and fast, as the flavor of coffee and whipped cream that always came with Mark flooded my senses and made me groan.

He kissed me with the tenacity of a starving man, and I ran my fingers through his hair as I opened to allow his tongue entry. As our tongues massage each other I couldn't help but squirm under the need to have him.

When he pulled back breathlessly to tell me to stop. To tell me no, and put an end to this again. I pleaded.

"Please-," I begged and pulled his lips to mine for a light kiss. "Please-," I begged as tears filled my eyes. Something in his face changed and I saw the Mark from before all this had happened before the worry lines and heartache.

"Shh," Mark quieted me and he leaned forward and kissed my lips, this time he was slow and methodical with the way he grazed his hands up and down my clothed body. He treated me as though I were a delicate flower.

I felt his fingers slide into the edge of my shorts and push them down as he leaned over and kissed my neck. He lightly nibbled on my shoulder when his fingers rubbed that tight bundle of nerves hidden by the apex between my legs. I gripped his arm and held on for dear life as his graceful touches were leaving a burning trail across my body.

"I love the way your body has always been ready for me," Mark spoke with a silvery tone as I lifted my leg to rest on his hip and give him more access.

"I love the way your skin flares when it needs me, and the way you suck air in through your teeth when you try not to make a sound," Mark gritted out and I stared into his eyes as my heart and clit raced to a similar rhythm.

He was merely going to get me off with his fingers, and that was not what I wanted. I wanted to taste him, to have him, to hold him, and to make love to him even if it was just a fleeting moment in time for him, it was everything to me.

I pushed his hand away and pushed him to lay down. I ran my hand down to his jeans and unbuttoned them. Mark put his hand on mine as I pulled the zipper down.

"Brooklyn, I," he started to protest so I ran my finger down and pushed it inside me as my juices flowed with a renewed need for Mark. It was a brazen move, but one that kept him right there with me as his eyes never left my finger as I coaxed myself closer to the brink.

"Sure you don't want this?" I asked as I brought my finger back up and slipped it into his mouth. He gripped my finger and encircled it with his tongue. He was giving me the green light.

I climbed under the comforter and reached inside his boxers to find a familiar sight. His large cock was ready and waiting for me. I immediately reached out and licked the moisture off the tip of as I heard Mark call my name. I then sank him into the back of my throat and swallowed.

"Fuck," I heard him gruffly say, as I set a relentless rhythm to show him what he was missing with Maya, and the feel the raging fire explode through my body that I didn't even get close to with Derrick.

"Your mouth is perfect," Mark growled. I knew what I was doing was wrong, and Mark knew it too, but there was something unfinished between us. No matter how many words were said, it stayed there like an invisible string pulling us together. In the morning, we would face the music, but here tonight we belonged to each other.

I moved my hand up and down his long shaft to match the rhythm of my mouth as I created a hot vacuum with my lips. I took my tongue and circled his head and then took him to my throat and swallowed again. I felt hands on my head as he showed me that familiar rhythm he needed to get where he needed to go.

"Fuck, Brooklyn," Mark groaned as I cupped his balls in my hand and massaged them. I moaned as I felt him swelling in my mouth. I could envision what it would feel like inside me, and juices coated my thigh as my clit reminded me that it needed more too. I pulled him out with a pop and pulled his pants and boxers off.

"I love feeling your dick swell on my tongue," I whispered, as I licked the head again. I needed more so I used my hand to continue rubbing up and down as I sat up over his cock. "Tell me no," I whispered as Mark watched me move to sit up over his cock ready to impale myself on him.

Mark said nothing as I put the tip of him in.

"Do you want me?" I asked as I tightened down on him forcing his fists to clench the sheets.

"Fuck, Brooklyn," Mark gritted as I slid a little further. I waited as my body expanded for his entry and he looked at me.

"Yes! Fuck I have to have you!" He growled as he took my hips and pushed me down. It burned as he pushed into resistant flesh. He was deeper in this position and it took a little bit of movement to get situated to the bite and pleasure that his cock was stirring up.

I unbuttoned Mark's shirt as he pulled mine over my head. There we were once again, nearly naked and needing each other as if our next breath depended on it.

I leaned forward and kissed Mark as he helped me find the speed to go as I moved up and down on him. My pussy walls vibrated their happiness as they swelled so I could feel him everywhere. He was in my body, my heart, and my soul at this very minute.

"Mark," I said and he merely pushed into me a little faster holding me in place. Sweat broke out across my body "Mark," I bit my lip as my toes curled and he smiled like a Cheshire cat, as the goosebumps followed. "Mark," I clamped down on him in hopes to stay my orgasm a little longer. It couldn't be over that fast.

"Shh, just let go. I will be here to catch you," Mark muttered, and I gripped his shoulders trying to hold out.

The fire had started the second he had touched me, and traveled across my body but as my tongue reached out to lick his scar he pushed up into me sharply and it broke my hold. My orgasm knocked the breath from me and left me chanting his name. Mark continued his relentless onslaught into my body as I rode wave after wave of fiery bliss. I slumped over on him sated, and he laughed.

"You really needed that," he stated with a smile while I caught my breath. I nearly cried, as the emotional overload had hit its maximum limit. How could Mark so easily get me here when Derrick couldn't even get close? Was I going to be forced to live an orgasm free life? *That would suck.*

"Brooklyn," Mark started as he wiped my tear. He sat up with me still impaled on him and pulled me to him. "Do you want me to stop?" Mark asked and I shook my head.

"I need you," I whispered and Mark leaned forward and pulled one nipple into his mouth. I sucked in a breath at how sensitive everything was, and when he bit lightly, I pushed my nails into his skin. My renewed need flourished as he used his hot mouth to suck the nipples of my ample breasts.

My body undulated as he laid kisses everywhere. He pulled my arm and place a kiss on my scar before running his tongue along it. I nearly combusted with another orgasm at the electric feel of him touching me there.

As I ground into him my clit grazed his flesh. I could feel him everywhere as that rough patch behind my pussy got exactly what it needed to say I wasn't done.

"Mark," I called out and then bit down on his neck as I tried to stifle my scream at the new charge running through my veins. I had never felt anything so intense. My nails dragged claw marks across his flesh he groaned, and I spiraled my rhythm to something sporadic, but I had found euphoria.

"Fuck Brooklyn, you are perfect," Mark murmured as his erratic breaths raced to match mine.

I clamped down on him, as lightning shot through me and he swelled even more. Mark sucked my other breast into his mouth as I continued to ride him. I felt his hand reach around and his finger circled the forbidden hole.

I flashed to the night that the line was crossed and the feel of both men inside me. I cried out as he pushed his finger into me and I cried out with the memory of seeing Mark give me everything he had while I opened the door for another man to be somewhere Mark had never been.

"Do you want that?" I grit through my teeth.

"Shh, let me give you what you need." Mark rasped out as I threw my head back at the feel of him everywhere.

"Mark," I cried out as he pushed harder into me in both holes. My movements grew even more sporadic as his sped up. I was going to erupt into sensual bliss.

"Fuck," Mark growled, as he pushed into me and fiery tingles ravaged my body before the fireworks exploded inside my veins.

I screamed as wave after wave pushed into me as Mark drove the climax to keep coming with each push into me until he found his own release. I leaned my forehead over on his as we tried to slow our breathing down.

"Wow, and here I was actually worried about Brooklyn," Maya stated as she stood in the doorway holding a take-out bag. *I needed to get an alarm for my door.*

Chapter Eighteen

"Maya," Mark yelled as he lifted me off of him and grabbed his jeans. "Maya wait," he called after her.

I got up and put on my black yoga pants and my white racer top, and walked into my living room. He had said he was going to tell her about the last time, but something told me he didn't.

"You bitch," Maya shouted as her fist connected with my cheek. That was the moment I found my spine as if she had shoved it back inside me. I grabbed her and placed her in a headlock and held her there.

"Listen to me," I demanded as she tried to pry herself loose. "I can do this all day long," I warned as she fought me harder.

"Brooklyn let her go," Mark shouted and the two detectives burst through my door with guns drawn.

"Maya if you will listen I can let you go," I spoke softly as the men seemed to group together to watch.

"Fine," she growled and I let her go to see the ring on her hand open up a cut on my arm when she swung at me. Rage enveloped me as I stared at the red blood flowing down my arm and covering Mark's name inside my tattoo.

"You hit like a fucking girl," I screamed as my brain saw nothing but red. I punched her across the face three times. She grabbed my hair and I screamed as she ripped some out. I punched her in the stomach and watched as she doubled over. I turned to look at Mark and she climbed onto my back.

I spun around in time to see my dad's men charging into my apartment with their guns drawn. *How many men does it take to break up two women fighting?* I grabbed her legs as they wrapped around my waist and fell backward landing on top of her.

Maya groaned as she laid on the floor and I got up and stared down at her. I placed my bare foot on her throat and Mark spoke up.

"Brooklyn, don't," Mark chimed in and I looked down to see Maya's lip bleeding as tears streaked her face as the bruises I had left on her developed across her body. I reached down to help her up as she slapped my hand away with my hair still in her fingers.

"How could you?" Maya asked as she sat up and looked over at Mark. He came forward and picked her up off the floor. He carried her over to my couch and sat down. I turned around and started waving the men back out of my door.

"Maya, I am sorry. Brooklyn is my kryptonite. When I am with her it is like we are drawn to each other, but we only wind up hurting each other and those we love," Mark stated. I turned to look at him as he enveloped her in his arms.

I watched as he pleaded with her and the love for her poured out of his eyes. I remember when he used to look at me that way, but it had been decades since I had seen it.

"You promised me you were over her," Maya's voice sounded soft and brittle as she struggled to pull herself together.

"I am over her. It is you I love," Mark spoke softly as Maya shook her head as if she didn't believe him, and why would she? She just saw the love of her life balls deep inside me.

"Maya, can I talk?" I asked as I sat on my coffee table and faced her. She sat silently and glared at me. "Mark is a great man, a wonderful man," I started and she sneered at me.

"Go get your own great and wonderful man," she spat my words back.

"It has been really difficult for everyone since I returned. Especially for Mark. We left so many things unsaid and undone when they told him I had died. Now that he knows I am not dead those things we should have said and done flare up, and it makes us vulnerable."

"You came back for him," Maya growled and I realized that it may take two to tango, but it only took one to carry the blame.

"It is my fault. I had a nightmare and I pushed him till he couldn't say no," I spoke softly without looking at them. "It only happened the one time, and won't happen again," I lied.

"Brooklyn-," Mark started, but I held my hand up as the blood dripped from my arm onto the coffee table.

"Maya you were completely right about me. *I am a whore*. Mark can tell you I slept with the District Attorney because I could while we were together. I even broke your trust sleeping with Mark tonight. Hell honey I even slept with my Marshal," I paused as Mark's face turned into a murderous stare. I had done nothing wrong, it wasn't like he was mine.

"You may be upset now, but for a man like Mark he is worth repairing the relationship. Give him a chance to make it right."

"How do I know you won't come for him again?" Maya asked and I understood her anxiety.

"Because I will be dead," I spoke in a whisper and both her and Mark stared at me.

"Brooklyn, I won't-," Mark started and I cut him off. I placed my hand on Maya's knee and looked her in the eye to show her I was serious.

"I will be dead and you won't have to worry anymore," I shivered as saying it out loud made it real.

"Mark is not going to let that man kill you," Maya spoke up in defense of Mark and his protective instincts, the problem is she was wrong.

"You would think that, but you were not the only one in this apartment without permission tonight."

Mark and Maya turned their heads to look where I was looking. The island in my kitchen had a box on top with a note and a blue forget me not. It was staged with care meaning he had been here for more than a few minutes.

A chill racked my body and I blew out the deep breath I had been holding.

"Brooklyn," Maya started as tears refilled her eyes. "I am sorry that you are going through this, but if you come near Mark again, I will make RJ look like a teddy bear."

"Take care of him," I whispered as I stood and walked over to the window. I wrapped my arms around myself suddenly feeling very alone in all this.

I picked up my phone as Mark had leapt into action and men once again came bursting through my door.

"Stevens," Derrick answered and I stayed silent as I watched the circus over a box on my island. "Brooklyn?" He mentioned my name and I hung up. I didn't know what to say. He always told me I was never alone and when I felt that way I called him, but I couldn't bring myself to ask him to come.

The police called out their crime scene investigators and they opened the box to find a photo of me freaking out with Taylor as the man dropped the rose on me.

There was a note that read:

YOU ARE FINALLY STANDING ON YOUR OWN. THOUGHT YOU WOULD ENJOY THIS PIECE OF YOUR

DADDY. ROUND TWO HAS STARTED, LET THE FUN BEGIN.

Under the photo was a piece of flesh encased in a plastic case. It was skin from my dad's shoulder it said "zakat nad Brooklyn."

"What does that say?" Detective Chase Matson asked, and I looked up at his blond hair and flawless face. I wonder if he had ever seen a crime scene with the lack of worry lines on his face, but shook the thought that they would place me with a new detective.

"The sunset over Brooklyn," I replied and Mark looked at me. "It was what my dad said about my mom, and how I got my name. He got that on their tenth wedding anniversary. My mom had the same tattoo."

"It was also in the Cut-Me-Not notes from last year. I have copies of all the files if you need to review them," Mark retorted making this less personal.

"How are you, Miss Montgomery?" Detective Jaxson Monroe asked and I smiled at him.

"Same ole shit, just more of it," I forced a laugh as my nerves were shot and shock had presented itself.

"You seem to be taking this extremely well," Detective Matson pointed out.

"She usually does before she does something incredibly stupid," Mark spoke over them, and I glared at him.

"You mean like the stupid thing we were doing an hour ago." Mark narrowed his eyes at me, and Maya sat on my couch watching everything unfold.

"Brooklyn, I think it is time we call Derrick and get you placed," Mark bellowed over all the people as I walked toward my bedroom.

"Not a fucking chance," I replied and when I got to the doorway, I turned back to see Mark was already texting him. "Send that text and you will be missing a testicle before the sun rises."

Maya glared at me, and the three detectives stared at me in their own version of shock as I had just threatened an officer.

"Brooklyn I can get Taylor to get another court order to place you in custody," Mark spoke up and my stomach dropped.

"Taylor is the one who had me placed with the Marshal's?" I asked as I stepped back into the living room.

"Yes, that was me," a voice shouted from my doorway. "You would never have gone on your own and it was for your own safety."

"You knew I was alive and lied to everyone?" I growled as anger started to boil inside me.

"You left me no choice Brooklyn. We loved you and didn't want to see you die," Taylor tried to break it down, but it only made rage envelop me

"So instead you shipped me off, like a kid going to boarding school and told those who didn't want to see me die that I was dead?"

Taylor picked up his phone and replied to a text and I knew what was coming. I knew I had just lost my freedom, but they were going to have to find me to get me.

"I feel completely betrayed," I murmured as Kate and I walked across the pier. I had hidden myself at an old house my father used when he needed to have private meetings with his men. It had only been a few days, but I was still bitter.

"Taylor knew I was alive and said nothing. He just sent me away. I knew there was a court order, but I expected it to come from the higher ups, not the man I shared a bed with just days earlier. Fuck Kate, you know I agreed to be his bitch and do whatever he said to let Mark go free, and he still sent me away without talking to me."

"I can see why you are so upset," Kate whispered as I continued.

"He has known where I have been all along," I let out an exasperated sigh as I continued. "Then Mark, the only man who seems to be able to get me hot and bothered, who said he was going to do the right thing and tell Maya what we had done hadn't said a word, and that lead to a fight between Maya and me."

"Yea about that the black eye you are sporting, it's sexy," Kate giggled and I rolled my eyes.

"You should have seen her bleeding and lying on the floor," I snickered as we walked back and forth in our secret hiding spot. It was a small strip of beach next to the ocean that the pier hid with rocks and pillars at each end.

"What are you going to do?" Kate asked as the sun glistened high over the water making the waves dance in the light.

"I have put a lot of thought into this," I started as my new black hair with blue chunks flowed in the wind. "I am going to go after RJ. I need to get back into my apartment to get some of the paperwork I was working on, and then the hunted will become the hunter."

"How are you going to get back into your apartment?" Kate asked and I smirked.

"I won't need to yet. I am going to call Derrick and ask him for help. I will burn in hell for this, but I am going to have him bring me some clothes and stuff, and then I am going to give him me. If he believes he is with me, he will be less likely to listen to Taylor. Plus, I can tell him I am thinking of where I want to go next."

Kate gave me the look that said she disagreed with what I was contemplating, but I had three men I needed to play a role and only one way to get them there.

"Maya is still not talking to Mark so they are taking a break while she calms down so he is technically single."

"What are you going to do with him?" Kate asked with a worried look on her face. I took a deep breath as my mind toed the line between right and wrong. I paced the beach thinking about my options, but soon my steps would slow as the answer became clear, and there was no avoiding it.

I explained my plan to Kate, who stared at me as though I had just murdered someone.

"Well, I can say this about you. You may go to bed a whore, but the next morning you will be my hero," Kate laughed.

She pulled me in for a hug and I welcomed it as I was feeling very alone in this. Mainly because I had people hunting for me for different reasons.

"I am so proud of you Brooklyn. Not for using your body as a subway ticket to get where you need to go, but I am proud to see that you are stronger than you were a year ago." Kate spoke softly as we laid down in the sand and soaked up the sun. I told her my secrets and she gave me the support I needed to move forward.

"I am after all my father's daughter," I whispered as I enjoyed this moment with my friend. "I know how to manipulate people to do what I need them to. It is unfortunate that I will be hated after."

I had to get one thing off my chest, and I took a deep breath as I moved forward to tell Kate how much I loved her.

"Kate listen to me," I started and she sat up and looked over at me while I stared at the ocean. "If I should die-," I started and she cut me off.

"Don't," Kate demanded. "I can't lose you again. You need to find a way to live through all this."

"Kate, I have people hunting for me to kill me, to protect me, and to send me away. I have to accept the real possibility that in my attempt to get away from the security personnel that I am opening myself up to an attack from RJ."

"Brooklyn, I can't talk about this."

"Just listen," I shouted as Kate stood up. "I want a silver casket with no flowers. I don't want a flower within a fifty-foot radius of me. I want an open casket. No matter how bad it may be, I want the world to see it is really me inside there. If I am not in there, then you never stop looking for me. If I am dead I want to be buried with my mom and dad. I want you to visit me once a year for a picnic of Chinese food and wine while you tell me about the next delicious actor you drooled over in a movie."

Kate wiped tears from her face as she stared out into the ocean. I didn't want to die, my journey to the depths of the ice cold ocean showed me that, but I had to accept reality. I was not invincible.

"What are you going to do now?" Kate asked as I stood up and wrapped my arms around her.

"I am going to get help," I replied and walked away.

Chapter Nineteen

It took forty minutes and four cabs to deliver me to the front door of my dad's house. I had to keep stopping and changing cabs to make sure I wasn't followed. I thought Anton had been taking care of the house, but the vines on the fence said no one was here. I pushed in the key code and the fence opened as the cab pulled inside. I paid the cab driver to wait while I looked around.

The porch was still blood stained from Cricket when I had found her. I walked up and shivered as the memories invaded my core. I put the key in the lock and opened the door as my mind flashed to the moment I found my dad lying behind the door. I stepped inside the silent house as my heels echoed off the white floor.

Someone had cleaned the house and it looked just like my dad had kept it, but it was eerily silent. I went upstairs and into my old room.

I had forgotten how bright and colorful my old bedroom was with pink walls and purple, black, and blue butterflies on the wall. I sat my purse on the black comforter with hot pink books drawn on the cover. I scanned the room noticing that nothing had ever changed. I walked over to my teakwood dresser and looked at the photos taped to the mirror that sat on top.

The first one was of Kate and me at our first middle school dance. I was so excited that we were finally becoming grown-ups and could go to dances. Mark, of course, was photobombing in the background by giving us rabbit ears.

The second photo was one of Mark in his football jersey with Kate and me in our cheerleading outfits from the night we won state. The three of us celebrated for a full day after and then crashed hard at Mark's parent's cabin. His parents died returning home from that trip a few days after we returned.

I wiped the dust off the photo frame on my dresser of my mom and dad who looked so happy with their daughter in pigtails and her friends at the beach. Mark and Kate had been part of my life from the beginning before anyone died, before anything was bad, before anything needed to be forgotten.

I was drifting down memory lane when I heard a noise and reached for my gun that wasn't in my purse. *Shit*. I had left it in Mark's SUV and never got it back. I took off my heels and hugged the wall behind my door.

"Brooklyn," Derrick's voice called out from the hallway. "Brooklyn honey you have a tracker in your purse."

I opened the door and allowed him to walk into my room. He looked around at all the bright colors and smiled.

"What?" I asked automatically annoyed for no reason.

"I never pictured you as the type to go for books and butterflies. I envisioned kickboxing stands after hearing about your fight."

I looked away to hide the black eye I was still sporting.

"Mark told me that you got tired of being called a whore and you finally gave Maya a piece of your fist." Derrick spoke softly as he moved around me to see that I was still a little swollen.

I watched as Derrick seemed to study my trophies from being an A+ student.

"You were smart," Derrick smiled as he turned back and smiled at me. He walked over and sat on the bed as I took the chair from my desk and spun it to face him.

"I see it as a testament to how much fun I didn't have. I was always inside the books unless Mark and Kate were dragging me out somewhere."

"Why are you here?" Derrick asked and I knew at some point he would want to know.

"I am meeting someone here in a little while, and I need you to be gone when they get here."

"Sounds covert," Derrick teased and he patted the bed for me to join him. I got up and slowly walked over to the bed and sat down beside him.

"One of my dad's men. He will bail if he sees you and I want to talk to him. I want closure for what happened here," I lied.

"Who was the first boy to kiss you?" Derrick asked changing the subject.

"His name was Eric," I burst out laughing, and Derrick motioned his hands to tell me to spill what was so funny. "I remember he kissed me and ran, but he ran straight into Mark and well Mark was mean back then. He gave the boy a wedgie so bad that he was walking around with underwear on his head."

Derrick laughed along with me, and he placed his hand over mine. I was comfortable with him here, but I wasn't in my apartment. *So weird.*

"First boy to take your virginity?" Derrick asked and I blushed.

"Mark," I replied and Derrick brushed the hair off my shoulder.

"Really? I didn't get that I-conquered-her-virginity-vibe from him. I only picked up on the you-hurt-her-and-I-will-kill-you-vibe."

"I doubt he remembers it," I spoke softly as Derrick pulled my blazer off and laid it on the bed.

"Honey every man remembers the cherries we pop," Derrick replied, but I knew better.

"We don't talk about it. We-um-It wasn't long after Mark's mom died and my dad went to prison. We were both hurting, but then my mom got sick and she died. We just kept taking blow after blow and there was nothing we could do to stop it. Mark and I needed an escape from it all. We planned out this trip to Vegas. We were going to elope and run away where no one could find us and give us any more bad news."

I froze not knowing if I wanted to dive any further into it, but Derrick turned me to face him and took both my hands in his and lightly rubbed in a circular motion.

"I told my aunt I was staying with Kate and we flew to Vegas. We got a room at the Palms, and went down and had a few drinks. Back then they didn't card like they do now. It was a lot more lenient."

A stray tear fell down my face with remembering the chain of events, but I wanted to tell Derrick. I wanted to let him in.

"Mark got drunk and we headed back up to the room. My aunt called Kate and told her my uncle had died in hospice care, and Kate called the hotel and told us. Even running away bad news had found me. We talked and decided getting married and running away wouldn't solve anything because it would always find us."

I stood up and walked to the window. I could still remember sitting on the hotel bed having to tell him someone else close to us died. I remember the look on his face as if he had killed my uncle himself. I could still see the anger in his eyes as he paced the floor.

"What happened?" Derrick asked and I turned back to look at him.

"I waited until Mark and I had processed it all and I decided I was sick of bad things happening, so I took Mark by his hand and I led him to stand next to the bed. Then I dropped to my knees and whispered the words "teach me," and he drunkenly argued with me for about ten minutes about how it would ruin us."

I laughed as another tear ran down my cheek.

"He said that friendships like ours can't hold up when we introduce sex into them. Funny how I can see what he said being true now, but I couldn't then. I thought we could survive anything. *We were invincible together.*"

"Brooklyn, you were just a kid," Derrick whispered as he came and stood behind me as I turned back to the window.

"What happened next Brooklyn?" Derrick asked as his hands ran down my body.

"I told her to take off her clothes and get on the bed," Mark spoke softly as I spun to see him standing in the doorway. "I remember her shaking like a leaf in the wind because she was so scared, but she never once asked me to stop. She did everything I told her to without hesitation."

I looked at Derrick and over at Mark. I didn't know what this was, but I knew I was not going willingly to witness protection.

"Derrick, what is this?" I asked, and he smiled as he walked over and sat in my chair so Mark and I were across from each other.

"Mark what happened next?" Derrick asked as I stood there thinking back to those moments when as kids we crossed a line that had corrupted us to be drawn to each other for years to come.

"I started by getting her aroused with kisses and getting her used to the feel of my touch. Then I climbed down and stuck my tongue to her clit. It was the first time I had ever tasted anything so sweet. I knew I had to have more and I forgot she was a virgin as I devoured her and made her scream till she was hoarse," Mark's words were aimed right at my heart. My skin flushed with goosebumps as I could see exactly what he was explaining.

"When I heard her scream my name it was like doing crack. I had to hear it again and again. It never got old. Like new songs that are played out on the radio," Mark's voice got deeper as he got closer to me, and my cheeks heated with a crimson blush to see Derrick eating up the story.

"Mark," I spoke his name in a whisper and he walked closer and placed a finger on my lips.

"I climbed over the top of her and wrapped her in my arms as her body pulsed with having her first orgasm. When she was ready I spread her legs further apart and stared into her eyes to watch for a sign that it was too much or if she wanted me to stop, but instead she surprised me when she tried to push my hips into her bare mound."

I shivered as his words grazed my body and my pulse raced to catch up to my erratic breathing. Mark walked around me and stood behind me so I was looking at Derrick, who had a hard on listening to the story.

"Why are you here Mark?" I asked as I was getting the impression he was up to something.

"Do you want me to finish the story?" Mark whispered in my ear. "Or do you want me to tell you why I am here?"

"Both," I stated as I licked my lips, and tilted my head away to give him access to my neck that he never put his mouth on.

"See Derrick, she is obedient in bed. It is the only place she will ever be, but you have to get her there first. Women like Brooklyn are like fine wine's their flavor gets better with every sip, and you want her nice and juicy before you have that first taste."

Mark then leaned down and kissed the skin between my neck and my shoulder and I moaned and rolled my eyes back into my head.

"I can still hear her panting when I slowly pushed inside her tight, hot, wet pussy. Her pulses sucked me in deeper and deeper. I was careful as I hit resistant flesh, but Brooklyn wasn't having it. She pushed my hips until I gave in and tore right through it. She was never one to have anything really soft and slow. She is not glass, she won't break.

"I can still remember her eyes dancing in the light as I held completely still waiting for her to adjust to me, but Brooklyn didn't need any time at all. Her face lit up, it was like magic. I could see every emotion she was feeling and wanted to keep her happy at that very moment. I wanted to brand her with my rock hard cock, and she begged me to do just that."

I sucked in a deep breath as Mark untied my silk shirt from behind me and let it fall open so he had unfettered access to my back. He reached around and placed his hands on my breasts as Derrick watched and I was helpless to do anything to stop him. I wanted him more than my next breath.

"Mark," I groaned as my head fell back on him as he toyed with my nipples. He was making them hard enough to cut glass as my body wiggled for more.

"Tell him Brooklyn," Mark whispered. "Tell Derrick what happened next."

I moaned as words had ceased to exist for me. I closed my eyes as he sucked my ear lobe into his mouth. I felt my pants being unbuckled as Mark's hand went up to wrap around my throat. I groaned as he squeezed a little.

I felt my pants drop as Mark's hand tightened down and his teeth grazed my neck.

"I pushed into her tight pussy over and over again, until she couldn't stop flailing with a need to orgasm. Remember that Derrick, she is a squirmer. I had to roll her on top of me and allow her to ride me. She was never one to just lay there. Even on her first time she didn't hold back as she rode me until I was seeing stars."

Mark's hand tightened down a little harder on my throat and everything he had said went in one ear and out the other. As Derrick stood in front of me and pushed his hand into my panties it felt like acid on my flesh and I began to fight.

Chapter Twenty

"Back off man," Mark growled and I fought to get lose from Mark. "Brooklyn, breathe," Mark whispered in my ear, and I tried to relax. I tried to come down, but I couldn't. "Derrick take a walk for a minute."

Mark then spun me in his arms and held me tightly as I cried on him. It was official I was fucking damaged and it was showing in my favorite activity. Mark lifted me and carried me over to the bed and coddled me as my fears and paranoias fled my system through my tears.

"Talk to me, Brooklyn," Mark demanded and I looked up at him. "You have never freaked out when I have done that."

"Why Mark?" I cried.

"Why what?" Mark looked at me in confusion.

"A year ago you left me because you couldn't share me and now you are trying to break me in for someone else. Why couldn't you just love me? What is so wrong with me that you can fuck me, but I get no respect?"

Mark stood up and left me to redress myself on the bed. I could see that I had pushed some button as he clenched his jaw in anger.

"I can't fucking be with you because I can't lose you. If you are already gone then I don't have to feel the pain when RJ kills you," Mark bellowed across the room. "You never fucking listen to anything we ever say and it is going to get you killed. I didn't give a shit that you wanted me to share you with Taylor because I would have given you the fucking planet. If that was what made you happy I would have shared you with an entire fire station, but it hurt."

Mark then turned to look at me and his eyes were red-rimmed.

"You really are my kryptonite Brooklyn and if you die, I will die. I felt you slipping away and it gutted me. There is nothing wrong with you, you are perfect, but I can't be with you because I can't survive if you die."

"Why Derrick?" I asked as tears flowed from us both. I had lost him so many times but each time it was like being gutted.

"He can save you," Mark replied as I saw the goodbye tear flow down his cheek. My big bad alpha's weak spot was me. "He can take you away from here and give you kids and a life that I can't."

I couldn't breathe with seeing how much pain I had caused Mark. I was in complete agony.

"Hate me if you must Brooklyn, but be grateful that I was man enough to admit I am not strong enough to survive you," then Mark walked to the door of the room. "Brooklyn I will always love you. I will always come running when you call. I will always be here when you need me, but I am begging you to go with Derrick and live.

Mark walked out of the room and out of my life. I fell into my pillow and cried. How many times would we say goodbye? Was that the last? My plan was ruined as I was pretty sure I would never see Mark again.

I woke up lying on my bed when I heard a door shut. I must have cried myself to sleep. I heard the back door again and sat straight up out of bed. I reached for my purse to realize I didn't have my gun. *Shit.*

I tiptoed into my parent's room. My parents had a hidden safe behind the wall in the closet. I turned the combination which was my birthday and took out a 9mm. I flicked off the safety and pulled back the slide to see it was loaded. I was ready.

I slowly walked down the stairs as I heard a voice talking. Old memories flooded me as I was careful to miss the steps that creaked and came down beside the stairs to the kitchen entryway. I peeked around the corner and saw someone sitting at the island.

"I do not want to spill your blood today, but I will." I spoke loudly as I rounded the corner and pointed the gun at the back of the gray head that sat at the island in the black marble kitchen.

"Moy Angel spoken just like her father," The man said as he turned around. I nearly fainted at the sight of my father's face on his twin brother Anton. In the soft light from the sun rising he was identical to my dad, and it made me shutter.

"Anton what are you doing here?" I asked keeping my gun aimed at his head.

"Come, sit. We talk about it." He offered in his thick Russian accent that left me pining for my own dad. I noticed that Kaleb, my dad's right-hand man was standing near the back door and gave him a half forced smile.

I lowered my weapon and walked over to the island. I scanned the cabinets and found fresh coffee grounds in the refrigerator. Looks like someone was staying here after all. I turned on the pot and then set out three coffee mugs while I waited for it to brew.

"You look so beautiful, like your mother. Moy Angel," Anton spoke sweetly, but I was in no mood.

"I just woke up and I haven't been your angel in a long time, Anton. You spent nine years in prison because some woman broke your heart so you broke her face," I spoke with disdain. Some things in my life no matter how different were still the same. I had as much angst toward him as I had my dad before he died, but I didn't care to fix that with Anton.

"I am a changed man," Anton spoke as I poured the coffee in the coffee cups. "Angel why haven't you come out and seen me? You know we are family," Anton sipped at his coffee.

"Why are you both here? I only called Kaleb," I asked as I gripped the handle of my gun.

"Why don't you trust me? I would never hurt you," Anton spoke as he stood up from the island.

The word trust was a broken one. I didn't trust anyone anymore. That is part of the default status my brain went to.

"You still mourn your father?" Anton asked and I nodded my head as I walked out toward the front door.

"I think it is not your father you mourn this morning, but rather Mark's engagement."

Anton and Kaleb followed as I went outside and breathed in the air as the moisture thickened from the humidity that was growing for the coming storm. Those words "Mark's engagement," came as a shock and cut like a knife.

"Anton, you don't know him like I do. He is happy with her," I walked over to the swing that hung from the tree in the yard and started to swing. I had wanted to come home I reminded myself. I wanted my freedom and with it came a price.

"Brooklyn, you are too much like your mother. When you get angry or upset you don't listen, you tune the world out. You forget right from wrong, and you behave poorly. Going after a killer is not the answer."

"How can you know about that?" I asked, but looked over to see Kaleb avoiding my direction.

"Brookie, you need to stop thinking about going after this man who killed your father. You are not immortal. This is too risky."

"Ten years ago you would have cut off his nuts for looking at you, but now you tell me it's too risky. Why? Because it's me going after him and not you?"

Anton stayed quiet as he walked behind me and pushed me in the swing as the sun began peeking over the buildings in the distance while the opposite direction showed a brutal storm headed our way.

"Brooklyn, I do not think you are thinking this through. You are not upset about the battle scars you carry from a killer. I think this is about the fear of losing people, and not being in control of the situations we get placed in."

"Anton you just don't get it. He killed my father and then for a year I thought my friends were dead. We all carry our scars and while I know RJ did that to us, I blame me. He took my life from me, and that doesn't go unpunished."

Kaleb's eyes lit up with the knowledge that my new found freedom was leading toward vengeance.

"Are you planning to go after him on your own?" Anton asked as he pushed me a little higher.

"Yes, I plan to kill him."

"Are you doing this because you think it will end your war or are you doing this because your heart is hurting?"

I didn't answer and Anton pulled my swing to a halt and knelt down in front of me. He picked up a little dandelion and held it before me.

"Brook, what do you think when you see this flower?" Anton asked.

"I see a weed that grows everywhere," I replied.

"Devochka Moya, do you see that you can blow on it and make a wish as the seeds drift into the air?" Anton asked then he blew the seeds off the flower. "Do you see that it is packed full of vitamins and minerals and can help save your life?"

"No, I don't see any of that," I replied wondering where he was going with this.

"You need to let the police do their jobs and live your own full life. You need to find someone who sees that you are full of wonderful things and doesn't see you as just a weed. You need to settle down with someone and stop chasing killers who will hurt you. One day it will be you in the casket if you are not careful." Anton dropped the remainder of the flower on the ground as the winds picked up and darkness began filling the sky.

"Anton," I started, but he kept talking over me.

"Brooklyn, I promised my brother to keep you safe. I want you to go back with the Marshal's and have a new life. You have to understand you are my only niece, you are supposed to bury me. I shouldn't have to bury you, and if you do this, I believe I will be standing over your grave to change the flowers very soon."

Anton turned and looked at the incoming storm and I watched as his chest rose and fell with deep breaths. Then he turned back around and pulled a piece of paper out of his pocket.

"Anton,

My time is running short as I have finally met an enemy I won't raise a hand to. I will succumb to his sword to save my daughter and allow her to have another day.
When you get out find my love and tell her, I am sorry. I am sorry for the life we gave her as she deserved to have two good parents instead of one.

Tell her I apologize for interfering with Mark. I truly thought she was too good for him, but I see them now and I see he would die for her.

Tell her that I am going to join her mother in the sky if the angels will have me and that I will always watch over her and protect her no matter where I may wind up.

Tell her the pain of regret is worse than the pain of heartbreak so she needs to go after the things she wants and never look back. Never second guess her choices.
When her final day comes, I want her to go peacefully in her sleep as an elderly woman with no regrets as to how her life turned out.

Tell her I may always be her Nikolas, but she will always be my Moy Malen'kiy angel (my little angel).

Anton watch over my daughter as if she was your own.

Niko

I sat in silence as Anton walked back inside the house and Kaleb came up and pushed my swing. My dad had known RJ was coming for him and instead of running or arming his men he came to terms with it and said his goodbye.

"Anton may not help you, but I will," Kaleb whispered and I smiled.

"You always were my favorite," I replied softly as we brought my swing to a halt.

"I love you Brookie, but this is about your father. He took me in when my own family didn't want me. They cast me out as a child when I told them I was gay. Your dad took me in and was my dad. Now I can never repay him, but I can help you stop his killer."

I nodded and walked back inside for my shoes and purse. I was going to grab the go-bags my dad had made up when we were younger to get us out of the country and then Kaleb and I were going to go discuss the plan.

I had already been here too long and I would be caught soon so I rushed to get everything. I got the bags and then went into my bedroom to see a little blue note flapping against my purse from the window that was open.

"You are not ready, but time is running out!
You know when and where.

Wear blue to match your hair and the flowers that will line your casket."

"Looks like RJ is growing a conscious if he is giving you a warning instead of a threat," Kaleb replied as he was waiting for me to leave.

"RJ didn't write this, someone else did. RJ doesn't have a soul."

Chapter Twenty

I stared at the map until I was going cross-eyed. I got up and put on a pot of coffee inside the cabin Kaleb had moved me to. I pulled out the coffee grounds container and looked at the new logo that said established in 1936.

I dropped it and ran back to the map, and looked at the year. It was a current map with current geological locations, but things had changed since RJ started killing people. I opened my laptop and started searching older maps. I found the one I was looking for from fifteen years ago and then looked at the current one.

I suddenly knew what I had to do to complete the plan, and it wouldn't make me a good person, but I did have half of my daddy in me so I could pull this off.

I picked up my phone and placed a bunch of calls. Then I went back to my apartment to shower and wait.

Three hours later I had everything in position and was ready when a knock sounded on my door and I opened it to see

Mark walk inside the apartment. He looked at me from head to toe as I stood before him in a black lace corset with garter straps holding up my thigh highs and black high heel shoes.

"Get out, go take a three-hour dinner," Mark growled at the cops that had joined me in my apartment.

"Take your friends with you because it is going to get loud, and make it five hours," I spoke up and cocked my eyebrow in a challenge at Mark. He merely smiled and showed me those cheek dimples I loved so much.

He came toward me, but I put my hand up to stop him.

"Do you feel guilty cheating on Maya?" I asked buying a little time for the policemen to leave.

"Want to talk about Derrick?" Mark retorted and I narrowed my eyes at him.

"What about him?" I asked and Mark smirked as he circled me.

"Want to tell me how big his cock is or how many times you screamed his name? If you want to open the door to Maya, we get to talk about Derrick as well."

"Mark," I whispered releasing a rush of air as he played with the strings of my corset. "I called you here to scratch an itch, but if you are not up for it," I challenged. "Your turn!"

"I really should feel guilty Brooklyn, and I would if it was anyone else, but you are in my soul while she is in my heart." Mark walked up and lifted my face to his and looked into my eyes as he spoke softly. "I know you love me Brooklyn, but you should know that I proposed and she said yes."

"Tonight I am not worried about the ring she wears because I know where your cock will be," I retorted and Mark looked at me inquisitively. He looked over me to see my laptop open and maps marked off on the coffee table.

Mark was a great detective and if I baited him with enough clues, he wouldn't leave till he was at the bottom of it. I smiled internally as he leaned down and placed his lips on mine, as my heart fluttered with the need to have him. I started unbuttoning his shirt when a knock sounded on my door. I pulled away and walked to the door and opened it.

"Wow, do you always answer your door like this?" Taylor asked. Then he took in Mark with a half unbuttoned shirt and looked at me with confusion. "What is this?"

"Brooklyn what is this?" Mark asked and I waved them inside my apartment. I went into the kitchen and poured a strawberry margarita for myself and made them both a scotch.

"This is sort of a contest to see who orgasms the loudest," I replied as I handed them their drinks.

Taylor and Mark looked at each other and then returned their look to me.

"Seriously?" Mark asked as his arms crossed and he took on that alpha tone.

"This is what I call Brooklyn getting her groove back. Derrick is all tied up at the moment and I need to know that I can finish my mission," I replied.

They both walked into the living room and were whispering as I chugged my drink, sat it down, and walked into my bedroom where I turned on my IPod. "Worth It" by Kid Ink came on and I started dancing. It was my new personal theme song.

I saw them watching me as I danced to the song. I walked over and grabbed Mark first. I dropped my body down his as I moved to the beat. Then I spun around and pushed my ass into his hardening groin. Mark grabbed my hips and pushed into me as he started to dance along. I swayed my hips to the drums and threw my arm behind his neck as my body undulated with his.

I shivered as he bit down on my neck between my ear and shoulder. Goosebumps broke out across my body as his hand came around and pressed into the flat of my stomach. He pushed me right up against him to feel every move he made as we rocked our bodies to the beat.

I shook my hips and slid down Mark's body to the beat. When I came back up his body, I spun around and reached for his shirt. I pulled him in for a light kiss. His familiar coffee and whipped cream flavor enveloped me and flooded me with memories that made me moan. I repeated it only this time when I went down his body as the ultimate tease I placed a kiss on his belt.

Taylor was behind me in an instant. He pulled me back up and pulled my hair to force my head back on his shoulder as he bit down on my neck. He swayed us to the rhythm as I moaned. His hands roamed down to the edge of my corset and his finger slid over my thongs as we rocked to the beat.

I looked at Mark and he knew I was up to something from the look in his eyes. I needed him to stop thinking so I reached over and unlatched his belt. I unbuttoned his pants and dropped his jeans.

Using my finger, I pushed him and allowed him to fall onto the bed. Then after he tore off his shoes and lost his pants. I sexy crawled over him until my mouth was face to face with his hardened length.

"Play along, or watch," I whispered to Taylor, who seemed frozen. They both knew I was up to something and had to work harder to distract them. I leaned forward leaving my ass in the air and placed Mark's head into my mouth and slowly slid down his length as I listened to him suck the air through his teeth.

I felt the Taylor's hands as he rubbed my butt and thighs. He seemed to be questioning this, but no man could resist a woman who was half naked and willing.

"Taylor, the more you play with me, the more I play with him, and soon the more I play with you," I stated with a wink and went back to Mark who eagerly grabbed my hair to put my mouth back over his cock as he pushed up into my mouth and I swallowed hard against him.

"Taylor, take off her thong," Mark chided as I slowed down. I smiled around his cock and knew that I was tasting freedom. I felt my panties get taken down my legs and lifted to allow him to get them off.

Mark and him shared some look and Mark pulled me as he scooted back on the bed. Taylor crawled up under me and place a kiss on my bare mound as he forced my hips lower until I was nearly doing the splits sitting on his face. I pulled Mark in and swallowed hard as I felt Taylor's tongue graze my clit. I moaned as my heart leapt into action and moisture flooded Taylor's face.

"Give him a taste Brooklyn," Mark called out and I screamed around his cock as Taylor pushed a finger inside of me finding that rough patch as Mark pushed harder into my mouth.

"Let him hear you," Mark demanded as he pulled me off his cock and Taylor grazed that rough patch again as he sucked my clit into his mouth. I tried not to make a sound, but Taylor's other hand reached up as he pushed two fingers into my ass without warning and I screamed out in need as he built me up the cliff.

"Mark," I called out and he merely smiled.

"Take it or tell us what you are up to," Mark retorted. This was going to be harder than I thought because he knew me too well. I dropped my head and sucked his balls into my mouth as one hand stroked his cock while I was being finger fucked from Taylor.

Before I could even think I was being lifted off of them and turned around. My ass was now facing Mark as my head faced Taylor.

"Try her mouth," Mark sneered and I knew he was baiting me to put a stop to this, but I was strung out and needed this orgasm as much as I needed them to participate.

I reached forward and pulled on Taylor's pants. I started to unbutton his jeans when I watched something flash across his face that threw me off.

"If you don't want to do this, you don't have to," I whispered in a challenge as I pulled him down to me, but whatever it was left his face as he pulled out this wide, hard cock. I leaned forward and licked the pre-cum from the tip and as soon as I felt Mark's tongue penetrate my pussy I sucked him in deep.

Mark knew me too well to know exactly what I needed and just how far he could push me before I would erupt. As I tried to curl my toes inside my heels and sweat broke out across my body, I felt Mark's tongue drag from my pussy to my ass and he licked the rim.

I twisted the bed sheet in my hands as my clit pulsed with the need to explode.

"Want me here?" Mark asked, but I gave no answer. I focused on Taylor as he was entirely too quiet. I cupped his balls as I heard a drawer shut. Within a moment, I felt my vibrator being placed inside my pussy, but it wasn't on. I clamped down on it needing it to do something.

"Taylor hold her hair," Mark called out and Taylor grabbed my hair. "You ready to tell us what this is about?" Mark asked and I swallowed down on Taylor until he groaned.

I felt Mark moving my juices up to my ass and knew he wanted to go where only Taylor had been before. The place that leaves you raw with emotion because it requires trust to allow entry.

"Trust me?" Mark called out and I said nothing. He wasted no time climbing up behind me and putting his cock at my entrance. "Trust me not to hurt you?" He challenged, but the truth was I did trust him to do whatever he wanted to me, that wasn't where the problem was.

He pushed in and I screamed as he made it through that ring of muscle. I continued to scream as the fullness and need to come broke out across my body in sweat. My skin flushed in crimson patches to show exactly how turned on I was. Mark knew what I needed, but left me hanging on the edge. The vibration in my throat had Taylor pulling my hair as he swelled in my mouth. I focused on Taylor as Mark gritted his teeth and pushed further into me. Soon Mark was all I could feel. Even with Taylor in my mouth Mark was all I knew.

Mark held perfectly still as Taylor erupted in my mouth. I swallowed him down and licked him clean. Then he popped out of my mouth and pulled his pants up. He leaned down and placed and kiss on my lips as Mark turned on the vibrator and I tightened down on him.

Taylor laid on the bed and pulled me over him as he sucked my breast into his mouth. Mark began his slow rhythm as he pulled almost all the way out of me and pushed all the way back in.

"What is this about Brooklyn?" Mark asked again.

"I need," I pleaded. I didn't think I would last. This was supposed to wear them out not me.

Mark pulled me up and kept my back to his chest. I was impaled on his cock and had nowhere to go as he held me still.

"Taylor," Mark called out and he moved up the bed and licked my clit that was pulsing loudly in my ears. "Make her come," Mark demanded and Taylor set a relentless pace on my apex. The vibration plus Mark being inside me left me squirming to get away or get more as Taylor worked at his own pace.

"Oh God," I screamed as I fought to get free. "Fuck," I chanted as I continued to climb up the hill of orgasmic bliss. Taylor pulled the vibrator out and Mark leaned me back so my pussy was directly in his face. Then he placed his hand over my throat and tightened his grip like before.

"Taste her," Mark growled in my ear. Taylor turned the vibrator on and pushed it against my clit as his tongue reached out to my pussy.

Fire started in my belly and flamed out across my skin. My toes curled and my fists clenched as Mark bit down on my neck. I screamed as the first wave shattered me into a thousand tiny little pieces and then came back to steamroll me. My body went on a heightened awareness of every touch and every lick.

"Who do you want to fuck you?" Mark asked and I chanted his name without a single thought in my mind. "Give us the room,"

Mark demanded and Taylor pushed the vibrator back inside me as he licked his lips.

"You are delicious," he stated as he gave me a kiss. "I will be back princess for more after I see what you are up to," and walked out of the room. He closed the door, and it was then that they had planned this just as I had.

Mark pushed me down to lay flat on the bed and came down on top of me. He pulled out and pushed back in as he whispered in my ear.

"You should know better than to think you can get one over on me," Mark chided as if he had won.

"I am getting exactly what I want," I replied. Mark pulled us up and turned me on his penis which was a new sensation that had me making a silent O. I was now facing him and those eyes who could tear me in two. "I only wanted to make you see what you are missing with Maya."

I leaned forward and placed a kiss on his scar as my hands grazed every ripple of muscle down his chest. I had to feel every inch because I knew after tonight I would never see him again. When he lost his rhythm, I took my tongue and grazed across the same flesh. Mark pulled my arm and ran his tongue across my scar and I screamed out. He was making sure I was marked to remember him everywhere.

I pulled his face to mine and kissed him with all the love I could pour into the kiss. I felt his velvet lips on mine and it coated my thighs with a renewed moisture.

"Where do you want me Brooklyn," Mark whispered and I knew I had him where I wanted him.

"I want you to claim me right where you are," I replied and his internal alpha came out and he lifted me up and down doing exactly what he wanted.

I felt his teeth on my neck as his hands gripped my breasts roughly. This was angry love-making, and I loved it. He reached down and turned the vibrator back on as we both felt it inside me, and he began pushing into me harder and harder.

"Come for me Mark, come hard," I growled as he pushed in and out of me so fast I could barely catch my breath. My orgasm rumbled from the darkened recess of my body and flourished me with need. I leaned over and bit down on Mark leaving a hickey as a reminder I was here.

I gripped his shoulders as my belly warmed with tingles and fire exploded in my nerve endings. I clamped down on him as tightly as I could as he pulled my hair and lightly bit my nipple.

I screamed silently as my voice gave out when my orgasm stole my breath. Mark growled as he came inside me, but he didn't stop pushing in and out of me, and it kept the waves of orgasm coming at me as I was lifted out of my body to see the magic being made and return in a blast to call out his name again.

"Fuck, Mark, I love you," I called out and he pushed into me one last time. "I know you do," he replied and that was all that needed to be said.

Chapter Twenty-one

After three rounds, I could barely move, but I had made a plan and needed to follow through. Taylor and Mark were both sound asleep in my bed with me in the middle. *It was like they hadn't gotten any in a year.*

I had waited until I knew they were both out before moving. I slid to the end of the bed and grabbed Mark's pants and took his handcuffs and cuffed his hand and Taylor's hand together over the bed railing.

I was careful not to wake them as the handcuffs went click. I then tiptoed to the end of the bed and took a photo of them sexed out of their minds and in bed together. I nearly laughed out loud with what I was doing.

I turned their phones off and put them in the toilet. *Oops,* I giggled quietly. I sent the picture to my printer which was attached to my laptop in the living room. While I waited for it to print, I took aspirin because my body hadn't been that used in a long time and I was feeling them everywhere. Being sore was an understatement. I then put on the jeans and black sweater and black Uggs, I had waiting for me in my go-bag and got dressed.

When the picture printed, I went and taped it to my television with a note that carried a timeline on when they could be un-cuffed without the picture being leaked.

I may have been a slut last night having two men in my bed, especially knowing one was recently engaged, but if this worked I would be the whore who saved the lives of many, and found justice for the victims and I was good with that.

I left a turn of the century map out for them as well as the case files. I knew them better than they thought as I laid out false paperwork. There was no way they were going to be one step ahead of me and know where I was going or what I was doing.

I put on my backpack, climbed up on my island and pushed the drop ceiling panel over as I lifted myself into the ceiling. I slowly low crawled through the dusty ceiling for what seemed like forever. Until I came to the large pipe that led to the rooftop fans. I took out my screwdriver and separated the pipes.

I was suddenly glad I had lost weight as I had to take my backpack off and push it up above me to get into the tight pipe. Fear enveloped me with irrational thoughts of getting stuck. I had to keep telling myself I had to move forward.

I was able to shimmy up to the fans and pushed the lid off that I had unscrewed days earlier as I climbed out. Those stupid fans hadn't worked in years and yet they were working just fine for me now. I walked to the edge of the roof and looked down to see that they had two officers in the alley. When I ran to the other side, there were two officers at the exit. Then there were four Marshal's sharing a smoke with a couple cops near the entrance.

I put on my backpack and took a running start as I jumped to leap from one rooftop to the next. I slid and landed on my hand which was throbbing as I shredded the skin, but I had to keep going. There was no going back.

I went to the roof-top door and knocked three times. The building manager Tony opened it and I gave him a thousand dollars.

"I was never here," I whispered and he handed me the gun I had lifted from my dad's house.

"I saw nothing," he replied and as I started down the steps, he spoke again. "Nice to see you being you, Brooklyn," he smiled and I returned it. This was as fun as it was scary.

When I got to the lobby, I watched as the fire department pulled up as they had been directly called for assistance with an elderly woman who lived below me. While the Marshal's and cops watched the firemen, I snuck out in the opposite direction of them.

I made it three blocks when I texted Kaleb that I was on my way. Then I tossed my phone in the trash and turned down an alley. Fifteen minutes later there was a black SUV waiting for me next to a park.

"Hey Kaleb," I whispered as I climbed inside.

"Hey Brooklyn, you sure you want to do this alone?"

Kaleb reminded me of a gruff Mr. Clean. He might have been my dad's right-hand man, but he wouldn't hurt a fly.

"No turning back now. I got this Kaleb," I spoke as I checked to make sure the gun was still loaded and ready. "Do you remember the plan?"

"Yes, as soon as you find me I am to take you to the airport. I have your passport and some more money that was stashed at your dad's house for you," Kaleb repeated the plan. In a couple of hours, the law would see me as a criminal, but I didn't see it that way.

Kaleb and I pulled up next to an old white beat up Cadillac that my dad had left in storage. My dad's men worked around the clock to get it running, because I would need to get away in something no one would be looking for.

"There is a storm moving in so make sure you are at the pier in two hours to get me," I declared as I started to get out of the SUV.

"Hey Brookie," Kaleb called out to me and I turned to look at him. "I am glad to see you have some of the Markovich blood running through your veins." I smiled at him.

"Today I am Brooklyn Tatiana Montgomery-Markovich."

An hour later I was parking the car next to an old dirt road as the rain started to sprinkle outside. I got out and used my flashlight from my bag to show me the way down the dirt road to the old gas station they had torn out.

I found the cellar doors to the gas tanks they kept underground. They were unlocked and uncovered. I knew I was in the right place. I tried to open the doors, but they were heavy. I looked around the debris and found an old shovel and a log. I used the shovel to elevate the door just enough to get the log in, but when I kicked a little harder holding shovel, the log fell all the way in and the door slammed shut.

I looked around and was about to give up as there was nothing else strong enough to pry those doors open with when I saw the lid of a sewer grate. I went over and lifted it off, letting it fall to the grass. I shined my light to see that there was standing water down below like in the photo of the girl he had sent. I pulled out my galoshes from my bag that were two sizes too big and put them on over my Uggs. Then I put the flashlight in my mouth and climbed inside.

As I dropped down into the tunnel, I shivered as I was now soaked to the bone. And the chill from the water I was standing in didn't help. There was a concrete wall between where I was and where I thought RJ might be so I walked down the darkened corridor careful not to get close to the sides where there were families of rats. I would make sure to call back and get someone to clear this out when my boots hit the ground in Paris.

"The Russian in you, must be what keeps you alive," a voice chided out and I cringed with the thought they had caught me. My heart raced and my breathing was erratic as I placed my hands on the handle of the gun in my waistband. "When you walk into a dragon's lair, you don't leave with all your limbs," The voice called out, but then I heard a muffled voice scream out in agony.

I peered around the corner to see a door that was partially open as it creaked with the flow of water. I walked up to it and saw someone with a cloak over their head and scars covering their body hanging from a chain while a man who looked like RJ, stabbed them again and again.

My heart leapt and my stomach revolted. I didn't expect to find a victim nor see what he did. I nearly vomited. I pulled out my gun and got ready to enter when a phone rang out.

"Bro, what's up?" The man answered the phone and I knew that wasn't RJ even though that looked like him. "What do you mean she is missing?" The man paced as blood dripped from a white handled knife.

He set the knife down on a contractors table in the front corner of the room and ran a hand through his hair. "Brooklyn wouldn't do that," I heard him say and I thought maybe it is RJ, but he had work done to his face again. "You expect me to believe that she was able to get away from the U.S. Marshal Service and the N.Y.P.D. without being seen?"

The man picked up the knife again and seemed to grow agitated with every second he was on the phone. I guess Mark and Taylor had woken up if someone on the outside knew.

"Fucking find her, this isn't the end game that was planned," the man was growing hysterical. "We are dead if she is dead so find her."

I watched as he threw his phone in anger and it bounced off the wall onto a table that held his tools as some slid off into water upon impact. He had his back to me so I slowly slipped through the open door and walked inside.

I was careful to stay in the shadows as I struggled to control my shaking as my skin turned to ice. The closer I got the more my heart sped up until it was all I could hear in my ears. I crouched down behind whoever was hanging as the man picked up his phone and dialed a number.

"Hey man, it's me," I held my breath when he turned around, but he was so distracted by his call he didn't see me. I held my breath until my lungs began to burn. I slowly let out my breath. "She escaped her detail again," I wanted to snicker that they had no clue I was here, but my fear wouldn't let me. "My guess is she was going back to her dad's place. Where else is she going to go?"

I noticed the lock was a key lock and looked around the body to see if I could see a key, but I saw nothing. I reached up and they flinched when I touched them to feel for a pulse. Their pulse was weak, but it was there as I heard labored breathing. They were walking the line between living and dying, but I couldn't leave this person behind as long as they were still breathing.

"That is why we put them there," the man stated as he put the phone on speaker.

"Listen, everything we did was to psychologically stunt her, so how the fuck did she grow a set to run off?" I knew the voice on the other line. That was RJ.

"Boss, what do you want me to do?" The man asked.

"Stay on track, and let me know when she turns up. Stupid bitch won't go far," RJ growled through the phone. "The wife is making us stay at the resort another day so when she does pop up leave her another note. She knows when I am coming for her, but it doesn't hurt to keep her confined to her apartment looking over her shoulder."

Then the line went dead and the man turned his back to us. I stood up and pointed my gun at his head. I was careful to keep control of my breathing so my shaking hand wouldn't miss my target.

"Where is he?" I shouted and the man turned around.

"Aren't you the smart cookie?" He snickered as if he had been expecting me. "I knew when I came on to the team that you were smarter than they gave you credit for, but you are weaker too. Which is why you won't pull the trigger."

The man took a step toward the hanging body and tsked me like the dragon, lion, spider and snake had done in my dream.

"I will put this fucking bullet in your brain, and not even flinch," I warned, but he smirked at my answer. "Where is he?"

I fired a warning shot into the wall as we encircled each other until he put the person hanging between us and I had no clear shot.

"You have until I get to three to tell me where he is," I ordered.

"One,"

"Brooklyn cutting off the snake's head won't kill him," the man said.

"Two,"

"Come on you won't shoot this poor innocent victim to kill me, right?"

"Thr-,"

"All right all right just wait," then the man pulled the cloak off and I saw my dad. He was barely alive, but it was him. He was skin and bones as tape covered his mouth and bruises covered his skin as it was lined with so many scars that his tattoos were barely visible.

"See," the man started as he stood up and walked beside my dad as shock was most likely evident on my face. "You can't shoot me when I have dear ole daddy."

Bang...

"I shot you because you did have my daddy you fucking imbecile," I shouted and I heard a child-like groan come from my father's lips. "Dad?" I called out, but I got no response and my father's eyes were shut. I had to find RJ and I had to get my dad help before he did die.

"Where is he?" I demanded as fury laced my words and remorse was a distant thought. The man cried as he tried to slither away, but his left leg wasn't working at all. "Next one is in your head," I shouted and the man screamed out.

"Vegas, he is on a company trip to Vegas."

"What company trip?" I demanded as the man cringed with every move he made.

"He owns a security company that puts in all the security cameras for the city. They do home monitoring and everything."

"What is his fucking problem with me?" I demanded answers but knew I was running out of time with the phone calls going out that I was missing.

"You were the love of his life, and you chose someone else," the man cried out.

"RJ is incapable of love and wouldn't recognize it if he saw it," I muttered as my hands shook with the realization I was going to pull the trigger really soon.

"RJ can't live without you. He killed these women because they look like you. He plays this game so you are always thinking of him," then the man began to laugh. "He knows everything you are going to do before you do it and watches while you do it. He will know you are here and know you shot me."

"He will know because I am going to leave his ass a fucking note," I retorted and pulled the trigger.

Bang...

A clean shot right through his forehead. I watched as shock enveloped me from what I had done. Blood poured out into the flowing water as I stared at what I had done. I was entranced until I heard a moan from my dad.

I went over to the body and hunted for keys, but he had none. I went to the desk and hunted for the keys, but the only thing I saw was the ballroom map for the upcoming policeman's ball that I was supposed to attend. Guess RJ was right I knew I would see him there, but I thought maybe I should ruin his vacation first.

I was running out of time. Without another thought, I spun around and shot the chain then ran for my dad. I lifted him up out of the water and pulled the tape from his lips.

"Daddy," I called out, but he didn't answer. "Daddy, come on please," I begged as my memory flashed to my begging Mark to live. "Nikolas," I called out and he cracked the tiniest smile.

"Ty krasivaya," he whispered.

"Dad I don't speak a lot of Russian. I have no idea what you are saying," I gritted as I tried to get him to stand up.

"Beautiful," he replied and I smiled at him.

"Can you walk?" I asked and he tried to get up on his feet but was too weak. We had to get out of there before RJ or his people figured it out, but first I wanted to leave a calling card.

"Dad I need to set you down," I whispered and my dad just gave me a crooked smile as I leaned him up against the wall. I reached into my bag and pulled out blue post it notes.

I decided to rhyme since RJ liked games. I hope he found the significance of it.

ROSES ARE RED
FORGET ME NOTS ARE BLUE
GUESS WHO SHOT YOUR MAN
AND IS NO LONGER AFRAID OF YOU.

I posted them in different spots. I probably could have papered the wall with notes, but when I heard my dad slump over it was time to go. I ran over and put my bag on the floor as I pulled gauze from my bag. I placed the gauze and then took the wrap off my hand and wrapped it around him as best I could.

I put my bag on my dad and draped him across me and took as much of his weight as I could. He must have weighed less than a hundred pounds now as I could nearly lift him without a struggle. I got him out the door and stuck to the shadows of the walls as his added weight made each step harder than the last.

The man's phone was ringing inside the room, and I had to gasp down anxious breaths as I realized they were going to know something happened. I had wasted too much time with the notes. I looked all around the pipes as I would never get my dad back up the tunnel I had dropped down into.

"Dad, I need you to try and walk with my help okay," I whispered as the phone started to ring again. My dad grunted and I lifted him over my shoulder and he held onto the wall. This was like being inside of a snake, and the dream reminder sent chills down my spine.

I tried to open a mahogany colored steel door, but it wouldn't budge. Just like my dream though a red exit door sat off in the distance. I knew if I ever reached it I would be slaughtered as my premonitions told me.

I sat my dad down and turned the gun on the lock and opened the mahogany colored door. These usually led me somewhere I didn't want to go, but no matter what I chose I had a 50/50 chance of survival. I heard a noise and gasped as someone was whistling. I backed up against the wall and prayed the darkness would shield us.

When the whistling passed, I kept walking down the tunnel until I saw a grate at an opening. I reached into my bag and grabbed my Gerber. I cut the zip ties on the door and opened it to climb out.

As soon as I was sure it was clear we climbed out and went straight for the tree line. I pushed my dad down behind a tree and covered the edge of his legs with leaves that were falling from the rain. I then crouched down behind another tree about ten feet from my dad. I tried to look for the edge of the dirt road, but I found myself hiding and saying a prayer as men were walking around talking.

"Someone better call the boss, looks like his little brother was killed in the tunnels, and the dad got away," a voice called out. "Oh, and you will love this, the dad left a note. RJ will be livid. That girl is as good as dead."

"I am not calling, you call," another said. "No, you call," they continued to argue until they were out of sight.

"Time to go," I whispered to my dad and threw his arm over my shoulder as I tried to run with him before anyone found us. I tripped and we both fell. His weight laying over me made it hard to get up.

I heard footsteps and pushed my dad off me and climbed over him to shield him when

Kaleb jumped out from behind some trees. He helped me off my dad and then picked up my dad. Then we ran for the car as fast as we could.

"What are you doing here?" I asked once my dad was lying in the back seat of Kaleb's SUV.

"Brookie, if you got in trouble you would have had no one. I have everything you needed but stayed here to make sure you came out. Anton would have killed me if you died."

"My dad needs help, and I need to get to Vegas," I replied bringing him in for a hug.

"I will take Niko to medsestra," then I shot Kaleb a look that said I didn't know what that meant. "I will take him to his nurse. There is a couple thousand in cash in the glove box of the Cadillac. Take this phone and I will call you with any updates," then Kaleb handed me a new cell phone.

"Thank you," I whispered as I looked in at my dad who looked as though he would be lucky if he made it. "Do we know anyone in Vegas that can get me a gun?"

"I can make some calls," Kaleb spoke softly and gave me a hug. "Now Thank me by returning with nothing more than his head," I nodded my understanding. So many of these men saw my dad as a father figure and wanted blood shed for what happened to him. I can only imagine what they would do to RJ if they found him after seeing my dad this way.

"Don't tell anyone he is alive until I return," and Kaleb nodded. As Kaleb ran around his SUV and climbed in, I opened the door and laid a soft kiss on my dad's forehead.

"No matter what happens daddy I love you," I whispered and Kaleb drove off after I closed the door.

I didn't have time to process that I had found my dad alive. I didn't have the mental capacity to process that I had killed a man, but he wasn't RJ. I had always been in the dark when it came to RJ, but with new information from the dead man about what he did and where to find him the rage in my veins kept me pushing forward.

I climbed in the car and headed straight for the airport. Come hell or high water I was going to get there and I was going to put a bullet in his brain.

Chapter Twenty-Two

I awoke to pounding on my door. I sat up out of bed and looked at the window, and rubbed my eyes. I had stayed in Vegas for a full week and found no leads, but loved every ounce of my freedom. Even threw the phone Kaleb gave me away on a layover in Denver. My electronic shackles had been broken for a two days and it felt amazing.

I came in on the red-eye and already regretted coming home. As the knock pounded again. *I just wanted to sleep*. I didn't want to face Mark, Taylor, or Derrick, but I would have to eventually.

"New York City police department please open the door."

The male voice shouted through my door. I closed my eyes and was eternally grateful it wasn't Mark's voice. I glanced at the clock again to see it was barely 8 am. I had only had about two hours of sleep. I grabbed my black NYPD hoodie and threw it on over my tank top. I should throw on some pants, but the pink shorts I had on were long enough that it didn't show too much.

I opened the door to see two beat cops in uniform at my door. One was holding a picture of me.

"Are you the Assistant District Attorney Brooklyn Montgomery?" The first officer asked as he looked at the picture his partner had in his hand.

"Yes, officer I am till Taylor fires me. Is there something I can do for you?" I asked sweetly.

"Are you alone in the apartment?"

I nodded my head and opened my door up all the way to show that I was in the apartment alone. The officer spoke into his radio telling them I was here. It wasn't a moment longer when I heard a familiar voice come through his radio.

"Arrest her!" My brain went into anger mode and stopped listening after the first two words. *Arrest me for what?* Before I could even think to speak, the officers were calling my name.

"Please face the wall, spread your legs and put your hands behind your head."

I complied. They would need to keep me behind bars to keep one of their own safe. When I got my hands on him, all bets were off. *He was having me arrested!* This was worse than the time he told my teacher I couldn't come to class because of hemorrhoids when I was in the principal's office with the flu. I was seriously going to maim him.

"Ma'am do you have any weapons or explosive devices on your person?" The officer asked.

"Take your chances and find out." I spat back out. They both whispered at each other. I was being arrested by newbies who had no idea what they were doing or what they were charging me with. They patted me down and put my hands behind my back and cuffed me. Then I was led inside my apartment and forced to sit on the couch.

"What are the charges?" I angrily yelled as they looked around my apartment. They had forgotten to even read me my Miranda rights.

"Let's start with resisting arrest." Mark's voice bellowed from the doorway.

"I haven't resisted," I replied and the two officers agreed as I shot Mark a dirty look.

"I thought you would at least make my job easy and put up a fight. Let's see if we can make up some charges. How about one count of evading police, one count of wasting tax dollars, and one count of pissing off the chief of police, the commissioner, and the mayor." Mark declared as Detective Jaxson Monroe moved around him with a smirk on his face.

"What about one count of extortion and blackmail for the photo you took. Another charge for damage to property since Taylor and I had to get new phones," Mark growled at me, but I refused to back down. "How about we just put you on suicide watch since you seem to have a death wish," Mark continued as I gritted my teeth.

"I merely went to Vegas," I glared at him, but Mark was even more stubborn than I was. He didn't even flinch.

"Can we have the room for a moment?" Mark asked and the two patrol cops along with Jaxson walked out into the hallway and closed the door. I was suddenly very aware that I was alone with Mark and handcuffed. I was at his mercy this time.

"Let's get something straight," Mark growled as he walked near me. It was like a lion's movements. Each step was thought out and premeditated, he was moving toward his prey as if he would pounce. "You left me handcuffed to Taylor and then photographed it and threatened to send it to the five o'clock news if anyone un-cuffed us before noon."

As Mark stood before me, I stood up off the couch and was only inches from him. I took in a deep breath and let my body feel the warmth and confidence that exuded from him. I had missed this; I had missed him. It had been a week since the last time we stood this close together, but the draw he had to me was still there and as strong as ever.

"Mark, please understand I had to."

Mark took a tiny step closer and stared down at me. I felt as though he was scolding me, but at the same time I have never felt so relieved to have him this close to me. I wanted to tell him everything, but I couldn't.

"Brooklyn, this entire week I have been doing my job non-stop. Half the city was out looking for you. We even had the geek squad scrolling through surveillance footage. Even the FBI was trying to track you. You never told me what you were doing or where you were going. You didn't trust me with whatever it was, and if you expect me to believe you went on vacation you are sadly mistaken."

"Mark, I am so sorry, but please trust me when I say I had to and when it comes to light, please know I have no regrets."

Mark quickly placed a finger on my lips to quiet me down, but I turned my head and continued. "I have to get this out. I know what I did to all of you was wrong, but it was worth it. What I gained from that was worth it."

I took a deep breath and closed my eyes. It was just me and Mark, the man I loved more than my own life. I didn't want to want him. I didn't want to need him, but even with Maya by his side I needed him to be there for me to unload all that I was carrying.

"Brooklyn, you didn't trust me to tell me in advance, you want to tell me now? Why did you handcuff us instead of telling us so we could be there to help you? What did you do?" Mark asked and I cringed.

"I can't tell you," I whispered and Mark looked shocked. "I would if I could, but I can't."

"Brooklyn, you can tell me anything," he retorted, but I couldn't tell him I had killed a man. I am sure he would find out soon enough, but I didn't want to tell him.

I closed my eyes so I didn't have to see the disappointment on his face. I opened my mouth to speak when I felt soft lips on mine, within seconds there was a hand around my back pulling me into him and his velvety tongue broke through to caress my tongue.

The flavor of coffee and whipped cream overwhelmed me and I wanted to grab him and pull him into me, but he was in charge and I was in handcuffs.

My body molded to his as it yearned to have him. My heart melted with each burst of flavor that he allowed me to have. I was powerless to his kisses and hungry for his body. I could only have what he gave and as he pulled away, I realized he had given me all he could. No matter what had changed from what I did it had never changed that I had broken us.

"Mark, I love you." I whispered begging my hoarse voice to return, and my rapid heart rate to slow as he released me.

"I know, Brooklyn, but you don't trust me."

I felt like it was a renewed stab in the heart. For some reason after finding my dad and putting the missing pieces of my life together I thought something had changed, but it hadn't.

"Mark, if I tell you what I did you will be forced to do your job, so trust that I can take care of myself and take care of Maya, she loves you."

Mark took a step closer to me and pulled on my handcuffs. He spun me around and released me from them.

"You're free, Brooklyn. You obviously can't trust me so do whatever you want! Just make sure your security team is with you at all times. Jaxson and Chase will wait with you while I go fix the mess you have left by running off."

I started to speak, but what would he say if I told him.

"Mark, I-," I started as butterflies took root in my belly. "I will tell you, but not here not now. If you want to know meet me at the courthouse tomorrow at 3 pm and I will tell you."

"I will think about it."

Then just like that he was out of my door. I felt hollow and numb, the pain had disappeared and there was nothing left. My life, my soul, and my body were empty. Everything in me was created because of knowing and loving Mark my whole life. My world was forgotten without him. Everything I knew to be real and true was a mirage of things I wanted to be real and true.

Jaxson walked over to the couch and sat down beside me as I held myself there with my hands over my face. He threw an arm around me and I went limp onto his chest as the tears fled my eyes.

"He loves you Brooklyn. He really and truly does, but whatever happened between you ended it, and you need to move on like he has so it doesn't hurt you anymore," Jaxson stated as he rubbed my back.

"I agree, whatever is happening between the two of you isn't healthy for either of you," I looked up to see the voice was coming from Detective Chase Matson. "I usually do not butt in, but let me tell you what happens when your mind strays from your heart. You wind up with someone you can't allow to know the deepest darkest parts of you. Then you lose them because they don't know all of you."

I stood up and walked to my bedroom door I was going to take a shower. Right, before I went to close the door I turned back to Jaxson to say something, but his phone rang.

"Monroe," he answered and I watched as his face slowly changed from serious to shock. "I understand sir."

Jaxson put down the phone and looked at me. He seemed to pause and clear his throat before talking.

"Miss Montgomery," Jax started and I cut him off.

"Call me Brooklyn," I whispered as he cleared his throat.

"Brooklyn, have you received any new threats? Letters? Flowers?"

"Why are you asking me this?" I asked as he now had my full attention.

"There has been a hostage taken, and they claim to be the real Cut-Me-Knot killer."

"That's insane, RJ never told us when he had a victim."

Jaxson's face fell and I knew something was very wrong. Mark chose that moment to come through my door and call for Jaxson, his face had fallen. Something big was going down, but the way they were already keeping me in the dark I knew it was time to get back into those tunnels.

Chapter Twenty-Three

"Taylor," I spoke softly when he answered the phone. "We need to talk; can you meet me tomorrow outside the courthouse at 3 pm?"

"I will be there, but you better have answers Brooklyn, because you are looking at serious charges of imprisonment if Mark presses charges.

Jaxson and Chase had to be at the Grand Jury the day after so I wanted to make sure I got everything covered today so I could ditch my security and take my dad and leave no trail. I planned to bail as they went into the courthouse.

"This better be important Brooklyn, we are convening the Grand Jury tomorrow," Taylor complained as I knew his workload was monstrous without me there.

"I am here," Mark's voice carried from behind me while I waited on the steps of the courthouse. "This better be worth it because I am so angry I don't want to even look at you."

"Alright Brooklyn you have me here, so what is it?" Taylor asked as I spun around to see him.

"It will be worth it," I whispered and we piled into a cab and drove off.

Forty-five minutes later we had gone four miles, but I had to make sure we were not followed and that we had lost my security detail. We pulled up outside of this tiny brownstone that was just over the river in Queens.

I knocked my special knock and an older woman came to the door.

"Eto moy otets zdes'?" I asked and the woman nodded. We walked inside and followed her into a kitchen where we waited a moment.

"What did you ask her?" Taylor asked and I smiled.

"I asked her if my father was here."

Both Taylor and Mark looked at each other in confusion and I was almost positive they were trying to decide what size straight jacket I would need, when she wheeled my dad around the corner in a wheelchair and I dropped to my knees to see him.

"How is this possible, Brooklyn?" Taylor asked as he kneeled down and I shrugged. "What did you do?" Mark jerked my arm back and looked at me in a serious manner.

"I murdered a man and stole my dad back."

Taylor stood up and paced for a moment and then sat silently in the kitchen chair as I fed my dad and washed his hands and feet. Mark stood stoic behind me in shock.

My dad was gaining weight and his motor skills were coming back slowly. He needed rehab, but I couldn't afford to put him in one where he would be found.

"Who did this to him?" Mark growled. I could see the same rage in his eyes that I had been feeling every time I thought about RJ. I didn't get a chance to answer as Taylor asked as the shock wore off. "Who did you kill?"

"From what I heard I killed RJ's little brother. I went to Vegas to kill RJ, but I couldn't find him. Now you know why he has a live victim, and it is my fault. I started this war."

"What do you want from me?" Taylor asked.

"Grant me legal immunity from prosecution for the murder."

"Why?"

"I need to be able to cross borders so when I murder RJ I can get my dad over the border without an arrest charge holding us here like we are sitting ducks."

"No, you are not running away!" Mark bellowed and my dad groaned.

"Brooklyn, I know we both went to law school so you should realize that if he had your dad then it would be self-defense," Taylor spoke softly.

"No, he claimed it as a residence and paid taxes on it therefore Castle Law applies and I am guilty of breaking and entering, trespassing, and manslaughter."

"Brooklyn we could argue you were acting as an officer of the law and this would be considered exigent circumstances." Taylor tried to argue it where I had done nothing wrong, but I knew what I had done and what the law says.

"Taylor that only applies if I heard my dad scream or knew he was in there. I didn't know until I had already trespassed after breaking in," and the room fell silent.

"What happened to the good girl who always followed the rules?" Taylor rhetorically asked, but I decided to respond anyway.

"The rules needed to be broken."

"But you won't break the law to walk away free?" Taylor questioned me.

"I still have my morals. I have to do the right thing now that I have done the wrong thing."

"Why didn't you tell me?" Mark angrily asked as his jaw clenched and those gorgeous blue eyes flamed with rage.

"You would have tried to stop me, or you would have been an accessory to murder."

"Where is the body?" Mark asked and I pulled a map and detailed notes from my back pocket and handed it to him.

"Brooklyn are you okay?" Taylor asked as I turned too fast.

"Yea just been a little dizzy lately. I may have caught a bug on the trip."

I walked over and sat in the chair at the table and sat beside my dad while my head stopped spinning and the nausea fell.

"Why Vegas?" Taylor asked and I looked over at my dad and he smiled for me. The nurse believed he had excessive nerve damage and didn't know if he would ever walk and talk again, but every time he smiled a crooked smile at me I knew I had done the right thing.

"I went to murder RJ. I wanted to do it before the ball," I explained and Taylor plugged his fingers in his ears and mumbled something about not being able to listen to it. "RJ is still coming for me, so I tried to get ahead of it, but I couldn't find him."

"Otdykh vremya," the nurse spoke up. Taylor and Mark looked at me for translation. I was really rusty at Russian and didn't know much so I was glad she didn't try to carry on conversations with me.

"We need to go. We have been here too long and my dad needs to rest."

I stood up and got really dizzy. Mark grabbed my arm and Taylor was behind me in an instant.

"Will you take me to Kate's?" I asked softly hoping Eddie was home. Taylor and Mark agreed and we started to walk out the door when the nurse came up and put peppermints and butterscotch candies in my hand.

"Beremennaya," she explained as to why she was giving me candy. She thought I was pregnant. That was insane I was on the pill. I stared at her while I counted the dates in my head and then I realized I had missed a period, but I was on the pill.

"What did she say?" Taylor asked and I did the math in my head which made me turn to look at Mark. He was standing there with a concerned look on his face. I could tell him she thinks I am pregnant and that I was late, but it wasn't the right time or place.

I always wanted Mark to want me because I was enough for him not because I got pregnant. Plus, I was trying to stop a killer a baby was not on the radar of things I wanted right now.

"She said it is for upset stomach," I lied. I would find out first and then I would never tell him because my dad and I would be in another country by the time I was showing. "Guys we can talk about this tomorrow, just meet me at the courthouse before the Grand Jury. I just want to go to Kate's and go home."

"You are preggers," Kate shouted from the bathroom. I inwardly groaned. "I am so excited I am going to be an aunt," she continued about how she was going to name it, spoil it, and love it.

"Kate I need to tell you something," I whispered while she was doing some kind of celebratory exercise that looked like an ancient tribe's rain dance. "I think you better sit down," I motioned for her to sit down.

I told her the whole story. Everything I had done, to include my trip to Vegas and how my dad was. I even showed her a picture of him on my cell phone and I watched as tears welled up in her eyes when she saw him,

"Will he be okay? Are you going to jail?" Kate wouldn't let me answer before she lunged at me and wrapped her arms around my neck. "I am going to get a complex about inspecting bodies at funerals after all of this," she whispered and I laughed.

I watched as Kate leaned down and placed a kiss on my belly and whispered to the baby. "When your mommy goes to jail I will raise you and teach you to be kick ass just like her."

"Kate!" I exclaimed at what she had said. "I know he is coming for me at the ball next week. I have to be ready."

"Brooklyn you have a baby inside you. You have to think about two of you now. Maybe now would be a good time to tell Derrick about your dad and he can make sure there are no charges and get you out of here."

"That is part of the problem, Kate," I spoke softly as I held a hand over my belly. "I have always considered everyone else. Everyone who looks like me is a target and now I am going to have a mini me. He or she will always be in danger if I don't kill him while I can."

"Brook you have to tell Mark," Kate rasped out as tears welled her eyes. She was overly emotional maybe she was pregnant.

"I am not telling him. I have gone back and forth with this. I love him and he loves me. I want him, but he wants Maya. If Maya and I were both to start running in opposite directions, he would follow behind her. One day if it is ever possible I will allow him to meet his child, but he deserves to be happy."

"Brooklyn, he deserves to decide what he wants," Kate replied as she stood up to emphasize how she felt about this with hand gestures. "I mean you can't keep this from him."

I stood up and pulled her arms down beside her body because she was making me dizzy.

"Kate, if I tell him, he will choose me, and he will want to raise the baby with me. He will come back to me."

"I am not hearing the downside to this right now, Brook," Kate scoffed.

"He won't be happy having to settle for someone he isn't in love with, and I will be miserable knowing that the whole time he is with me is because of a baby and not because he chose me."

Kates face turned a shade of crimson I had never seen before with her blond hair and pale complexion.

"Kate?" I asked as she seemed to be so angry she was speechless.

"Brooklyn, you tell him or I will!" She pulled out of my grasp and stormed into the kitchen. "My mom never told my dad and by the time I found him he had this whole other life. Don't get me wrong I love my step dad, but both my dad and I should have had a choice of if we wanted to know each other." She grabbed a bottle of water from the refrigerator and walked back over to me. She placed her hands on both sides of my cheeks for emphasis. "Tell him by the ball or I will!"

Chapter Twenty-four

"You ready?" I asked Jaxson as I watched him straighten his tie yet again. "You look fine you know."

"I hate talking in front of large groups of people."

"It is just a Grand Jury. All you do is go in and answer questions to the best of your ability," I spoke softly as I walked over and fixed his tie he made crooked.

"I'm good. Abbott and Costello are going to lead and follow us over to the courthouse. Chase is already headed over there. He wanted to talk to Taylor before they began.

I smiled and then walked into my bathroom and looked in the mirror. I was wearing a baby blue sleeveless silk shirt and a black pencil skirt with my strappy black heels. I brushed my hair that was once again all black and had curls on the bottom half. I looked ready to go to court.

"Let's go," I replied grabbing my purse and shoving a Ziploc of crackers and candy into it. I was not going to get sick there.

About a half hour later we were playing follow the leader with the cars as we headed up to the northern side of Manhattan. Halfway there we got a flat on the vehicle and the guys placed roadside wagers on how fast they could get it done, and had us ready to go in twenty minutes.

As we pulled up to the courthouse, I saw Chase coming out the doors with Taylor. Jaxson helped me out and I went with Abbott and Costello up to meet Taylor as they had broken for lunch.

I turned and waved at Chase as he and Jaxson shook hands and watched as Jaxson came running toward me when I heard the sound of squealing tires. I turned as my heart leapt into action looking for wherever it came from.

I felt Costello's body strum to life as energy seemed to charge him. Abbott grabbed me and flung me to the ground. Squealing tires sounded again this time near the sidewalk and shots rang out. My heart was racing as I was surrounded by testosterone. I had three hardened male bodies surrounding me and not in a good way. I felt as though I was being crushed as people screamed and panic flooded the atmosphere.

"Taylor!" I screamed out.

"I'm here honey. I am right here," Taylor reached inside my igloo of bodyguards and grabbed my hand. "You are going to be fine."

My hand was torn from Taylor's as I was lifted and carried back up the stairs of the courthouse. I looked over Costello's shoulder to see Chase lying on the courthouse steps and there seemed to be blood or something dark dripping down the steps all around him.

I saw Jaxson running for him as I was rushed through the doors and past security where I was placed inside a room where Abbott and Costello stayed by the door.

"Wa- was that him?" I asked as my voice trembled with my body. I felt like my heart was running a marathon that my body had not yet been invited to and was struggling to keep up.

I felt sick and stood up and grabbed a trash can. I started throwing up. Everyone was talking and moving around me that I just shut my eyes and closed everyone out as I got a handle on my anxiety and my nausea.

"Are you okay Brooklyn? Are you hit? Do you need an ambulance?" Abbott asked as I finally allowed the conversation to absorb into my ears.

"I am fine," I whispered as I hugged the trash can. "Was that RJ? Did that detective get shot because of me?" I asked without opening my eyes.

"No," Taylor's voice rang out from a side door. "That was not RJ. We can see them on the security cameras. That was a deliberate act against Detective Matson."

"How do you know that just from a video?"

"Brooklyn, Chase was working on something confidential for us and had been getting threats. The people we were targeting shut down their websites at the same time he was shot and then posted a video of the shooting. This was not about you," Taylor whispered as he came over to rub my back.

I started hurling again and wondered if it was going to be this way every time RJ got my blood pumping.

"Brooklyn, maybe we should take you to the emergency room, you have been sick for days."

There was more chaos all around me, and I could hear them talking about me as if I wasn't present on what could be wrong with me and what I needed to do. I tried to tune them out, but it was getting harder as they were getting louder than the chaotic sounds of people screaming and sirens blaring.

"How is she?" Someone asked, then I heard "we are going to get her an ambulance she could be in shock." I couldn't take much more I just wanted them all to be quiet and get away from me.

"I am fucking fine!" I shouted over all of them and the room went silent.

"How do you know you are okay?" Taylor started in again with his debating.

"I'm pregnant! I am not in shock. I am not shot. I do not have the flu. I do not need an ambulance, doctor, or any of the above."

I hurled into the trash can again. The baby did not like it when I got angry or anxious. I can already envision how the next nine months would go.

Taylor handed me a napkin as I sat back in a chair to look up and see Mark standing over me with his arms crossed. He was waiting for me to say something, but all I wanted to do was sleep now that my body was coming down from the adrenaline.

"Maybe we should give you two a few minutes," Taylor whispered and ordered everyone to stand outside my door and keep everyone out of the room I was in until I could be moved.

Mark pulled out the chair and sat down across from me. I was sure from the tears I had makeup running down my face, and I probably looked like I ate a Gremlin, but I don't think he noticed because he seemed to be somewhere else.

The second hand clicked so loudly on the clock inside the room. Each new sound was a reminder that I needed to be talking to him or Kate was going to.

"I don't want anything from you," I whispered as tears filled my eyes from the overwhelming face-slapping emotions that came with that sentence. "I wasn't-," I paused and looked down at my hands. "I don't-," I never had any intention of telling him until Kate went all, 'Do the right thing,' on me so I hadn't worked out how I was supposed to tell him.

"Is it mine?" Mark asked and I nodded as a new tear rolled down my face.

"Hey we need any and all hands outside to help with the mass hysteria," a man yelled at us as he flung the door open. Costello ran in and pulled me away before anything else could be said.

Chapter Twenty five

"What does that mean for the baby?" I asked my doctor for the third time because I just wasn't processing what he was saying.

"This early in your pregnancy your HCG levels should be doubling every other day if not more. Yours have not. According to your labs, they were slowly increasing, but today you have a significant drop," the doctor spoke in a comforting tone.

I turned my head and looked at Doctor James Garie. He was the county coroner and my friend. He was a heavy-set man with a salt and pepper beard with a Santa belly. He always broke stuff down for me when I didn't understand.

"Brooklyn, you are most likely going to lose the baby," Doctor Garie placed his hand on my shoulder.

"What about my dad?" I asked for the ninth time because this was all a lot to process.

"Your dad had severe spinal damage. While we are still waiting to see if there was severe brain damage from oxygen loss I can tell you your dad will never walk again. He will be lucky if he can talk or hold his own fork. He is in a state of constant pain as both his skin and his organs have scar tissue covering them. There is a high possibility that he will never recover and need hospice care to help him with his final days."

"What does that mean for the baby?"

I was in a constant state of repeat. No matter what they said to me, it just didn't compute. I could hear them and I could repeat them, but their words sounded like a foreign language I had yet to learn.

"Brooklyn, honey can you hear me?" Doctor Garie asked and I smiled at him.

"I saved my dad to watch him die, and the stress from it may have killed my baby," I whispered as tears burned my eyes.

"Is there someone I can call?" The doctor asked and I looked at him as Doctor Garie kept an arm on me.

"No, there is no one to call. I am in this alone," I whispered and Doctor Garie gave me a look that said he knew I was lying. I knew I could call any of them, but I was the epitome of bad news. It followed me everywhere.

"James," I whispered as the doctor left the room while he could so he didn't have to repeat himself again. "Can you do me a favor?" I asked.

"Whatever you need Brooklyn," he replied.

"Get my dad into a private home under a different name. If he is in constant pain I want him somewhere we can manage it so he doesn't suffer. Then could you call Detective Stone and tell him he won't be a dad so he can get married without a problem."

"What are you going to do?" James asked as I climbed off the exam table.

"I am going home to rest," I replied and grabbed my things. James agreed to take care of those things for me and I gave him a hug as a way of saying thank you. He looked at me with concern but didn't question it.

Upon arrival at my apartment, there were two new officers at my door. I had never seen them before, but since Detective Matson's death it was all hands on deck to find the killer. The NYPD didn't tolerate you hurting one of their own.

I introduced myself and used my key to open the door and walk into my apartment. I walked into the kitchen and placed my purse on the island to see RJ standing next to my television.

His green eyes glimmered with excitement to see me. His black shirt and black pants made him look like a burglar, but his blond hair contrasted it to say look at me.

"What do you want?" I asked numbly. Normally I would be freaking out, but I was still in shock and I had a baby to think about.

"I thought we should talk," he replied and I cocked an eyebrow.

"What would we ever have to talk about that didn't come on a post it?"

"I thought we should talk about the meaning of an eye for an eye." RJ moved his arm to let me see that he was carrying that same white handled knife that he had murdered so many with.

"Are those your dirty cops at my door?"

"Yes, they work for me," RJ replied and pulled the knife from his holster. "Why aren't you quivering in fear like you have been for twelve months?" RJ asked and I shrugged.

"Believe it or not there are worse things than you."

"Really? Do tell," RJ chided as he moved closer toward me until there was only the island between us.

"I'm pregnant, and-," RJ's face shifted and he turned red.

"Pregnant was not part of the deal," RJ shouted as he seemed to be trying to control his rage. "That was not what we had agreed to."

I stood in absolute silence as RJ rattled on some psychotic rant about how he had agreed with someone I wouldn't get pregnant. I thought he had finally lost it. He didn't even see when I reached in the kitchen drawer.

"RJ shut the fuck up!" I screamed and he looked at the barrel of my gun

"Killing me won't end it Brooklyn" RJ rasped out. I cocked and eyebrow as I flipped the safety off.

"Wanna fucking bet?" I challenged.

"You need me, Brooklyn. You need me to be the go-between. I merely want to watch you scream in agony as I pierce your skin. There is a higher power who wants your head mounted to a wall."

I was too tired of running from him to even listen to the words he said. I had been through so much, but death would be letting him off easy. I aimed the gun at his waist and smiled at him.

"Brooklyn, you don't want to do this," RJ exclaimed as he covered his crotch with his hands. He danced around where the bullet could go anywhere.

"That is where you are fucked up RJ, you still think I give a damn about the words that come out of your mouth or the order they come out in."

Bang...

"Bitch, you shot me!" RJ screamed as his blood trickled out of his leg on my kitchen floor. He fell to the ground and I walked over to him and aimed the gun at his head.

"Did you get my note?" I asked sarcastically.

"Brooklyn put the gun down," Mark called out from my door. I looked up to see he was followed by about twenty other officers.

"I'm going to lose the baby because of him," I cried as I played with the trigger on the gun.

"It's okay Brooklyn, everything happens for a reason. Maybe you and I were not supposed to have kids, or maybe kids are supposed to wait until this guy is not chasing you anymore," Mark was trying to get me to lower my weapon. He placed his gun back in his holster as he stepped in and other officers flooded my apartment.

"My dad is going to die because of him." I continued as realization hit that not only was I a murderer, but two other lives would be lost because I couldn't stop him before now.

"Brooklyn, RJ is a bad man, but letting him die lets him get off easy. We should put him in prison and punish him first. Just put the gun down," Mark took a couple steps toward me.

"I have seen hell in my dreams and he deserves to be there with them," I yelled. "I have nothing left. He took everything from me."

"Brook, you have me. We ended honey he didn't take away our fairy tale romance. We did that all on our own, but that doesn't mean you lost me."

"You said it hurts you to be near me because I am going to die, because of him," I challenged.

"Brooklyn, think about the live victim he took. We don't know where she is. If you kill him, she dies." Mark took another step as RJ's eye struggled to stay open.

"I want to kill him," I whispered and before Mark could say a word RJ reached up and stuck his knife into my leg. I pulled the trigger hitting him in the shoulder as I screamed and fell to the ground.

Within seconds, he was swarmed and paramedics were in the room. I saw Eddie come in and he put me on his gurney and carried me down the elevator into his ambulance. Mark climbed in the back with us as the sirens sounded and we headed for the hospital.

"Kate is going to kill me if you die," Eddie joked as exhaustion flooded me.

"Then don't let me die," I retorted.

"Brooklyn, this is not the time or place, but we need to talk," Eddie spoke softly.

"I won't be going anywhere for at least ten more minutes," I joked. Then I watched as Eddie pulled a box from his pocket and opened it. I looked over at Mark to see he was happy with it.

"I want to ask Kate to marry me, but she won't say yes without your blessing."

"You wait until I get stabbed to ask for my blessing?" I teased as the morphine made my skin feel ice cold, but my veins were running hot. "Eddie I could ask for a better man for my friend, but there is no guarantee she will be happy with him like she is with you. I will give you my blessing while on morphine, but you better ask again when I am sober," I whispered and he tried to hug me only to smother me.

"You are the best Brooklyn," Eddie cheered me on as the blood pressure cuff started to tighten my arm.

"You mean because I shoot bad guys, but yet I am humble?" I asked as the drugs overpowered my speech.

Eddie's face fell as he looked at the screen and he was no longer joking. I watched him scramble around and he put a monitor on my finger. My pulse was slow.

"Brooklyn, how do you feel right now?" Eddie asked and I shivered.

"I am tired, and cold."

"Stay with me sweetheart," Eddie shouted.

"What is happening?" Mark asked and Eddie merely looked at him. Then words were shouted into radios as Mark came into my vision in duplicate.

"Brooklyn, honey I need you to stay with me," Mark pleaded.

"You have Maya now," I whispered as my head felt heavy. "You want her not me," my mouth was instituting word vomit since the drugs took away my cognitive thinking. I turned my head as it got harder to breathe to see Eddie putting an oxygen mask over me and giving my IV a shot.

"Get her there now," Eddie screamed and I smiled up at them both.

"Everything happens for a reason," I muttered behind my mask.

"Brooklyn, don't go. Don't leave me," Mark shed a tear and while I knew it was serious, there wasn't enough energy left to be concerned.

"I'm tired," I spoke silently as my voice had disappeared.

"Brooklyn, listen to me. You are going to live because you are the stubbornest woman I have ever known. Your adventurous attitude and the ability to never listen drives me up the wall and into your arms. I have always chosen you because I always wanted you, but this moment right here kept me from keeping you."

I lifted my heavy hand and placed it on Mark's as the tears became more prominent as he spoke.

"Brooklyn, I lived an entire year without you and it was miserable. There is not another person on the planet like you and if there were I wouldn't want them because they would merely be a duplicate. This journey you have been on was unfair that you were targeted. It was devastating to everyone to be reminded every day that it could be your last."

Mark leaned over and kissed my forehead as darkness circled me.

"We are losing her," Eddie screamed as the monitor slowed.

"Brooklyn, I don't want to live without you. I want you to fight with me and demand I treat you better. I want you to call me on my shit and tell me to do better, to be better. I want to marry you and have babies with you, but I can't do that if you give up. Please Brookie, don't give up on me."

Chapter Twenty-six

"Brooklyn, I swear I am going to make you a freaking blond again if you don't wake up!" Kate yelled at me and I cracked eyes just a hair to see she was painting my nails and Mark was giving me a sponge bath.

"I can't let you make her a blond, but we could do hot pink. She would wake up just to cuss at us," Mark retorted as I felt tingles on my legs as he bathed me.

"Kate," Mark called out and I felt my hand fall.

"Don't yell like that, you scare me to death! What is your issue?" Kate asked as she picked my hand back up.

"She has goosebumps!" Mark exclaimed and I inwardly grinned at his weird observation.

"So," Kate replied as she picked my hand back up to finish painting my nails.

"Kate if she has goosebumps then she can feel us," Mark replied as a new wave of goosebumps flourished me as he placed a cool rag on my legs.

"You are seeing what you want to. Brooklyn will wake up when she wants to or when we dye her hair pink."

I used all my energy to focus on moving my fingers, and I heard a scream as I held up my middle finger on the hand she was painting.

"Mark, she is flipping me the bird," Kate squealed.

"Even in a coma she knows what your worth," Mark chuckled. It was the first sign of happiness I had heard in a while.

"Asshole," I whispered nearly silent and the room fell still.

"Brooklyn?" Mark's voice said my name as if it was a question. "Kate call the doctor."

I heard a loud beep and then a thick British accent.

"Nurse," I heard the voice say.

"We need the doctor!" Kate exclaimed.

"Is the patient in distress?" The nurse replied.

"No, she is flipping me off, and I swear she talked."

"I will notify him," then the room was silent again.

"Maybe we are finally losing our minds," Kate broke the silence. I wanted to say something, but everything hurt. I felt stiff like I hadn't stretched in months.

"Hi Mark and Kate, how is our patient this morning?" I knew that voice that was James Garie, the coroner, but I didn't know why he was here, I wasn't dead.

"She flipped me off, and called Mark an asshole," Kate nearly shouted. "But now nothing."

I felt a hand lay on my forehead and tilted my head into the warmth of the palm. It was the tiniest movement, but everyone went silent again. I saw a light behind my eyelids and closed them tighter. Then I heard a chuckle.

"Welcome back Brooklyn," Doctor Garie stated and I so wanted to say something smart-assed, but I couldn't even get my eyelids open.

"Why isn't she communicating?" Mark asked as Kate held my hand tighter.

"Maybe Brooklyn has nothing to say, or it could be that she is just bouncing back and her body is stiff from the lack of use. Her brain activity all came back normal so now it is up to her when she comes back," James spoke softly and laid his hand on my shoulder. I then felt his breath in my ear. "My dear, you might want to wake up before these two kill each other."

I inwardly smiled again. Kate definitely would make Mark's life hell every day that he was here, but that was just her being a protective friend.

There we scuffling noises it sounded like chairs being slid or someone was taking nails across a chalkboard.

"Brooklyn," Mark called my name and I tilted my head to the voice. "Brooklyn can you look at me, sweetheart?"

I really tried as I felt him brush my hair off my shoulders, but my body didn't seem to want to listen. I felt Kate take my hand in hers, and she gripped it tight.

"Brooklyn, open your eyes honey, please look at me," Mark stated and I tried, but my eyelids seemed to weigh fifty pounds.

"You are pushing her too fast, and going about this the wrong way," Kate whispered.

"No, Kate, saying hey bitch wake up would be the wrong way to go about it," Mark retorted. Then the arguing ensued. I listened to Mark say he knew me better, but Kate loved me longer. My heart rate was speeding up from the beeping in the background. I fought myself and everything that protested against me moving and opened my eyes.

Kate and Mark were blurry in the bright light. I closed my eyes and opened them again as they continued to argue over me.

"Shut up," I whispered, but it wasn't loud enough because it burned my throat. "Shut up," I tried again, but I sounded weak and raspy.

"Shut up!" I screamed and everything fell silent. Mark and Kate both started talking at the same time and I couldn't make out what they were saying.

"Water," I whispered and then Kate leapt off the bed and left the room. Then she returned with a cup of water and a cup of ice chips. It was hard to suck out of the straw without pain so Mark took the ice chips and began feeding them to me.

"Brooklyn, I am so sorry that you felt like you were never my first choice. The truth is you were my only choice. I tried to avoid it. I tried to let you find someone better, but I can't fight fate. I need you in my life," Mark spoke softly as he fed me the ice one at a time.

"Don't worry Brook, Mark and I have had a lot of time to talk and he knows if he hurts you again I will cut off his nuts, have them bronzed and hang them on my Christmas tree year after year," Kate whispered with a smile.

"That won't be necessary," Mark growled, and I wanted to laugh, but my face hurt. "How do you feel?" Mark asked.

"Sore," I spoke in a hoarse whisper. The ice felt heavy on my stomach and it was making me sleepy. I didn't want to go to sleep, but my body had other plans that I wasn't allowed to alter, and darkness took me under quickly.

"Are you sure I am ready to go home? I have only been awake a week," I asked the doctor as he explained that everything in my labs was normal.

"Miss Montgomery, it is time, and for what it is worth you have an amazing support team that will help you get to where you need to go. Just remember to lean on them instead of stressing out your body taking it all on your own."

I watched as the young blond haired doctor walked out of the room. I felt like his speech was some kind of subliminal message but blew it off.

I stood up and started getting dressed when my door opened. Mark walked in and helped me.

"This is a first," I muttered.

"What is?" Mark asked and I smiled at him.

"It is the first time you were putting my clothes on," I laughed and he smiled at me.

"You are my favorite bouncy castle princess," Mark smiled as I relished the smile on his face.

"Just as long as I am your only bouncy castle princess, mini golf mistress, laser tag lover, or go kart girlfriend," I laughed.

"What about my t-ball tramp?" Mark asked and I burst out laughing.

"You will have to outsource that because I don't play games where you have to hit the balls. I would much rather fondle them," I stated with a wink.

"You ready to go home?" Mark asked and my stomach dropped. I was nervous about going back there, but it should be fine. RJ was in solitary confinement pending his trial, and for once no one was chasing me.

"Hey Mark," I asked as I grabbed his arm. "Before we leave this place, I have one question no one answered.

"What is it?" Mark asked and I had his complete attention.

"The babies name. What did you name the baby?" I asked and Mark looked questionably at me.

"You want to hear this?" He asked and I nodded my head. "You were a few months along. You must have gotten pregnant that first night you came back. It was a boy, and I named him Nick after your dad."

"I like that name," I said with a smile.

"I happen to love that name," a voice called out from my door. I looked over to see my dad looking happy and healthy. His body was still scarred, but he was no longer skinny and weak.

"Daddy," I screamed as I went for him. He stood up out of his wheelchair and caught me as I ran for him. "How are you standing?" I asked as he pulled me into his arms.

"Lyubov Moya, the doctors don't know everything," My dad tightened his arms around me.

"Why didn't you fight or run before they did this to you? Why didn't you give up?" I asked flooding my dad with questions.

"Brooklyn," my dad's face turned serious. "I didn't run because he would have killed you. I didn't fight back because if he would have won he would have murdered you. I never give up because I am a Markovich. It is not in our nature. We may go about doing things in a oblazhalsya (fucked up) manner, but we get it done."

I pulled back and took my dad's hands in mine to see he had all of his fingers. I wrinkled my brow and flashed to the moment when the box was left and Derrick confirmed it was my dad's finger.

"What are you doing?" My dad asked as I moved his shirt sleeve to see his tattoo while severely scarred, was still intact as well. I then flashed to the moment we found the piece of flesh in the second box.

"Brooklyn, what is it?" Mark asked as I started hyperventilating.

"I need to see RJ," I spoke up and as the men protested I drowned out their voices with my own thoughts. It was all right there in front of me, but the puzzle pieces didn't fit.

"No, I am going to see him now!"

Chapter Twenty-seven

"Name and identification please," the guard asked, but I had never changed over to a Brooklyn ID.

"Call the Warden, or District Attorney Cross," I pleaded when I didn't have the means to get inside.

"Ah Detective Stone, how are you doing today?" The guard smiled at him and stuck her pen in her mouth. I was going to shove it in her eye if she didn't stop.

"I am taking her to see him," Mark responded formally.

"You know the rules detective, she needs to have ID or you need to buy me a drink," the guard giggled and I wanted to slap her. I was about to say something when Mark picked up the phone.

"John, its Mark," then I listened to formalities and football talk. Then he got to the point. "Your guard named Nikki won't let Brook in with me because she lost her ID."

Then Mark put the phone on the tray and slid it inside the opening for IDs. There was a lot of yelling and apologizing happening.

When she hung up she buzzed the door and we walked through the long corridor being buzzed through at least five more doors before we got to an open area.

They had moved RJ to a cage so I could talk to him. I could see him in the distance as a chill racked my body. As if he was in-tuned with me as I got closer and I met his eyes he smirked.

"Ahh my sunset has returned," RJ glared at me. He completely ignored Mark.

"How is the shoulder? The leg?" I asked sarcastically as I sat down across from him at the table.

"I am doing just fine, Brooklyn, but something tells me you didn't come to visit to see how I was doing," RJ smirked and leaned in and whispered "you know don't you?"

"Get away from her," Mark growled as he stood closer to me.

"The pieces don't fit," I replied and Mark shot me a look of confusion.

"Sure they do Brooklyn, twist the pieces until they fall into place," RJ gave me a Cheshire grin and I wanted to punch him in the face for all I have been though. "You know it is not over."

"You are in solitary until they decided to institute town hangings," Mark gritted his teeth. "It is finished."

"Let me see your scar, and I will give you a clue," RJ bargained. Mark protested, but I stood up and lifted my khaki pants and showed him the scar that showed up on both sides of my calves. "That was so worth this. To see my brand on your flesh."

"I'm waiting," I responded as I dropped my pant leg and sat back down.

"When Mark's mommy dearest was fucking my dad they had a son. This boy was born two years before I was. He was placed in foster care because neither of them wanted proof of what they had been doing, but the boy grew up wanting to know, and eventually he came to see me. I let him live in our basement, and he helped mold me into who I am today," RJ sneered.

"The finger? tattoo?" I asked as Mark was lost in the conversation.

"Our brother got it from someone," bells and whistles started sounding in my head and I knew just about everything I needed to.

"I don't have any half-brothers," Mark immediately went defensive.

"RJ, who is this man now?" I asked and he smiled.

"You should know, you already let him into your life and into your bed," RJ then called the guard. I felt sick that I had let someone so evil spend so much time with me. I never even saw it in him, there was never a single thing that told me he was bad, except... "The pieces fit, Brooklyn when you stop forcing it."

I was stunned, but I had thought about this moment, and while it wasn't in a courtroom like I envisioned it I stood up and turned around to face RJ, and as a final F-you to him I lifted my pants and peeled the fake scars off my legs.

"What? How?" RJ demanded as the guard came and opened the door.

"Miracles of modern science, and lotion," I smirked. "Thanks for the info your brother will be waiting for you in hell." I glared at him.

"You won't kill him," RJ chided.

"People don't kill people, guns kill people, and mine has the barrel of a bloodhound and will seek him out and put a bullet in between his eyes. So, no I won't kill him, but my gun will."

Then RJ was escorted off yelling as Mark looked at me in confusion.

"It's not over?" Mark asked and I knew I should have told him when the pieces started falling into place, but I didn't want to unless I knew for sure.

"I need to find Taylor, now!"

Chapter Twenty-eight

"Brooklyn it has been three days since we left the hospital. Don't you think you should rest?" Mark asked as he paced behind me in the basement of the courthouse.

"Quiet," Kate called out. "This is kind of more important than getting a little nookie." Mark and I both rolled our eyes, and I giggled. "What is so funny?" Kate demanded to know.

"An hour ago we were fucking over the table you are sitting at," Mark and I burst out laughing as Kate sneered.

"I think I found it," Kate called out. We all walked over to her to see an old marriage certificate annulment form.

"It says that Mark's mom Hannah and RJ's dad Curtis were too young to have been married. Mark's grandparents petitioned the courts and the church to reverse the marriage. The courts granted the annulment after the unnamed baby boy was born and placed with the state."

"What else does it say?" Mark asked, but the records were cut off except for one notation by the court clerk.

"There was also a daughter born and placed with the state eleven months after the divorce was finished."

"I have a docket number, but I would need Taylor to access it since he locked me out of the system. When does he return from DC?"

"He will be here the day after tomorrow," Kate replied as she looked at my phone that chimed while she was texting Taylor. "Umm, guys," Kate's voice shook and she turned her phone to face me.

"You should have let RJ kill you as his death would have been much less painful than the one I have for you and your boyfriend too. I don't play games so heed this warning, I am coming for all of you. Now run and hide if you can."

I snatched the phone back and decided I was done with this being scared bullshit. I typed a message back.

"You better bring it before I find you, because when I do I am sending you straight to hell."

"Really Brooklyn?" Kate asked as she read the message. "That is the best shit talking you have?" She shook her head and I couldn't help but smile. In light of a new threat, Kate was focused on my smack talking abilities, and not taking the new threat seriously.

"Run away with me," Mark spoke up and I turned to face him. "Run away with me to Vegas like we did as kids."

"Mark they are not going to hurt me," I reassured him. "I am not going to let this go on where I run and they chase. Bullies are only bullies until someone knocks them down."

Mark shook his head at me. I turned my head to see Eddie coming in to pick up Kate for dinner. I smiled at him and turned back around to see Mark on his knees.

"What are you doing?" I asked as he looked up at me. "Get up from there, what are you doing?"

"Brooklyn, shut up and let the man propose!" Kate exclaimed as she jumped up and down clapping and giggling. I wanted to laugh at her, but I turned back to Mark, who had pulled out a ring.

"What about Maya?" I asked quietly. "I knew we were still rubbing each other the right way, but where is she in all this?"

"Oh. My. God. You didn't tell her?" Kate squealed.

"Can I propose or do you want to do it for me?" Mark asked sarcastically.

"I-," Kate started in but a look went back and forth between Eddie and Mark and Eddie nodded before pushing her lips closed and when Kate tried to protest Eddie pulled her into his arms and kissed her deeply.

"Brooklyn the minute we started losing you I realized what a douche I had been." I smiled at him as his beautiful blue eyes told a story of how they always wanted to be facing me.

"When we lost you. When I watched, you die. I made a promise to you and to God that if he saved you. If he brought you back to me, I would stop being a coward. I would stop thinking I knew what was best for you, and I promised if you chose me I would take care of you every single day that we could share together."

Kate said "awe," in the background as my eyes filled with tears. I had wanted this, but I wanted it for the right reasons. Babies and fear of losing someone were not reasons to get married.

"When Maya came to the hospital, I told her I had always loved you, but I had been challenging and distant even when you gave me all of you. I told her I was going to spend my life gaining your trust, your respect, and your love. She left in tears, but came back each day and read a new book to you. She helped me take care of you for a while. Then finally she said goodbye. She could finally see that you were the only one for me."

I blew out a breath as my heart melted.

"How do I know that come tomorrow you will decide you don't want me anymore?" I asked and Kate started to talk, but Eddie put a hand over her mouth.

"You have to trust me," Mark replied and there was the problem I didn't know if I trusted him. I knew I loved him and was attracted to him. I knew I craved him and wanted to feel that pull that was between us. I trusted him to save my life and to take care of me when I was sick. I trusted him with everything else but did I trust him with my heart. "The only promise I can make to you is to give you all of me, and that if I fuck you from here to Sunday you won't wake up on Monday morning alone with a broken heart. You will wake up wrapped in my arms, and you will know how much I love you."

"Mark, I-," I started, but he pulled out a black diamond. This was not the ring he gave

Maya. This was not his mother's ring. "Where did this come from?" I asked and then heard a groan from Eddie when Kate bit him to get to talk.

"I went with Mark to get a ring that was not a hand-me-down or something that wasn't you. We spent nearly two weeks looking and finally a designer said he could help," Kate spoke with a huge grin.

I picked it up and looked at it. It was a black princess cut diamond on a silver band flourished in blue sapphires.

"The black diamond is because you love black and because of your beautiful hair. The blue is for your eyes, and then if you look, there is an inscription inside. Now Mark continue..."

"Thank you, Kate. Once more Shh," Mark growled and I chuckled at her insistence that he get this right.

I tilted the ring and looked at the engraved word inside. "Naveki moy," I stared at it because my Russian wasn't fluent enough to translate it. Mark took my free hand and pulled it to him.

"Even if you tell me no that you won't marry me that ring is going on your finger. It is beautiful and flawless like you and it says you are 'forever mine' inside. Don't make me one of these people who have to chase you Brooklyn. Make me your husband and live your life with me. If we have to run from psychos who want to kill you, then we will do it together. Marry me Brooklyn."

Kate was chanting 'yes,' as Eddie struggled to keep her quiet. I watched as Mark took my hand and he slipped the ring onto my finger and a tear fell from my eye.

"What do you say Brooklyn? Do you want to run away from bad people with me by your side?"

"No," I said and the room fell eerily silent. "I don't want to run. I want to hunt bad people with you as my husband."

Mark stood up and picked me up and spun me in his arms. He laid his lips on mine and I immediately wanted to get naked up against one of the bookshelves behind but chose to wait until we got home when Eddie and were not around.

"You just made the best decision of your life and I will spend every day making sure you don't regret it," Mark whispered as my feet hung a foot off the floor and he twirled me around with him as though we were carefree kids.

"Taylor's assistant Sherrie is waiting to drive my Escalade to the airport so the four of us can fly to Vegas if you want to get married tonight," Mark whispered in my ear.

"I can't wait to be married to you, let's go."

"Yay! I am so glad you said yes after I had to break into your apartment and pack for you," Kate stated as she wrapped her arms around me and whispered, "I love you so much."

Everyone walked up stairs and down the courthouse steps. I saw the bleached out blood stain from Detective Matson and made a decision that I was going to look into that as soon as we got back.

Sherrie walked ahead of us as we all laughed and shared our excitement for this trip that Mark had planned. We were talking about all the things we wanted to do when a red light caught my eye on Mark's SUV.

"Hey Sherrie," I called out and she turned back to look at me, but the light stood still on his car when she moved. "Never mind."

I ignored it and pulled Eddie back behind Mark and Kate.

"When are you going to ask?" I whispered, and he smiled.

"Vegas," he replied and I laughed. Then I looked to see that red light had moved and I looked up the buildings but saw nothing that would make that light.

"Hey Mark," I called out as they walked ahead of us. He turned back and I saw the light flicker. "Sherrie No!" I screamed as she turned over the SUV, and it exploded into a ball of flames. Mark and Kate were both thrown back behind us as Eddie and I were pushed to the road by the force.

I ignored the pain to my body and looked up to see Mark was bleeding from his head and was unconscious. Kate looked dead, as Eddie climbed up to rush to her side. I did everything Eddie told me to do while we waited for the ambulance.

They loaded them up and took them to the hospital where I was getting stitched up. I answered a thousand questions from the FBI, they had sent the two agents I hated the most, but I answered them without hesitation.

"Miss Montgomery," the doctor called out and Eddie and I leapt to hear the news of if they were alive or dead.

"How is Mark? What about Kate?" I asked immediately not giving him time to talk.

"You're the sister to Kathryn Harper, correct?" The doctor asked and I lied.

"Yes I am her sister, and this is her fiancé," I pointed at Eddie.

"She has a concussion and minor cuts and bruises. We are going to keep her overnight for observation, but she is very lucky."

I watched as he moved her chart and read something. Then he was pointing at the chair for us to sit. *Oh, God.* My stomach sank as I knew something really bad was coming.

"I am really sorry," the doctor started and I turned to puke in the plant. I couldn't breathe, my heart was racing in my ears and I couldn't hear the doctor.

"Brooklyn," Eddie shouted through the blood rushing through my ears. "Brooklyn, he's not dead." Eddie handed me paper towels the nurse had brought in as tears left tracks down my cheeks. "Brook, he's not dead," Eddie said again and I looked at the doctor.

"Miss Montgomery, I didn't mean to scare you," the doctor stated and I wanted to slap him. "I was apologizing because with the head trauma Detective Stone has no idea who he is. We believe it to be a form of retrograde amnesia. Which means he could one day wake up and remember everything, or he will never remember anything," the doctor stated in a rush as his pager went off. "I have to go, but the nurse can answer anything until I get back."

Then he was just gone. Eddie and I went to check on Kate, who was upset that she got blood in her hair. I f'ing loved that girl more than she could ever know. Twice she has nearly been killed and instead of letting it mess with her head she uses it as a learning lesson to always have clean clothes and back-up hair products with her.

We got Kate into a wheelchair that she was telling the nurses she was going to bedazzle because it looked like a boy chair and wheeled her down the hall to Mark's room.

I pushed the door open and we all rolled inside. I walked up and sat on his bed as he turned to look at me. His eyes didn't glow like they usually did. They didn't dance like I knew always had.

"Hi, Mark," I spoke softly and he looked at Eddie and Kate. They spoke their hellos as well.

"We're you in the explosion?" He asked and I nodded my head. "Did they have to tell you who you were too?" I shook my head.

"What is your name?" Mark asked and my heart broke.

"I'm Brooklyn," I whispered as I tried to keep my tears back.

I heard a phone ring and went in the direction of it. I opened the closet and pulled out Mark's phone.

"GAME ON BITCH! FINAL ROUND HAS BEGUN!"

<u>Upcoming releases:</u>

Water Wishes is anticipated to
release nov/dec 2015

Survived by Brooklyn –

The return of Brooklyn

Anticipated feb/mar 2016

Follow me here for updates:

www.Facebook.com/authorlizyork

Or

http://authorlizyork.com